LONGING FOR LOVE

Sunset Bay Romance, Book Three

DEBRA CLOPTON

Longing for Love

Sometimes a dream might need a rewrite…

Erin Sinclair's dream of running a successful B&B is on shaky ground. Her tiny inn is building a good reputation but needs more guests and more good reviews. When a *New York Times* best-selling author's agent books the honeymoon suite as a writing retreat, it is an opportunity to put the Inn at Sunset Bay on the map. *The* Nash Bond is coming to her B&B for two months and Erin can hardly believe it. But he has a reputation of being hard to handle when he's in the midst of a book. And he's reclusive, too. So what is he doing, coming to her B&B? And what if she's unable to satisfy him? What if instead of a good review, he gives her a terrible review?

Everything is on the line. Is she up for the challenge? She has to be.

Nash Bond needs this book. He needs to get out of the

slump he's in, but a year ago his life changed when he lost his adoptive father—his hero—and the words that had once flowed without worry suddenly dried up in his grief. Now his agent is shaking things up by booking him a special room in a special place—her words—and she insists he give it a try. She reminds him his publisher is getting impatient. He knows everything is on the line. He doesn't like it at all and when he meets the gorgeous, but pushy B&B owner, sparks fly. He's suddenly feeling things he's never felt before…but with his past, he knows all too well that longing for love leaves a person open to pain, thus he locked his heart away a long time ago and has no plans to change.

But on the shores of Sunset Bay, can romance bloom? Can love heal a broken heart and give him a happily-ever-after he never thought he wanted? Or needed?

CHAPTER ONE

Nash Bond pulled in front of the B&B and stared at it. So, this was it. His home for the next two months. He hoped coming to this small town on the beach to do the research for his new book would help get him out of this stall that he was in…he would *not* say "block." He didn't believe in writer's block. Nope, not him. He'd always said just sit your butt in the chair and write. No excuses.

He had no excuse; he'd been preaching that for years and had always said that you didn't get to be where he was in the writing business without believing it was a business and his job was to write. A bad page could be edited; a blank page was a blank page.

Junk could be turned into gold. He loved what he did, or at least he always had loved it until…he'd hit a wall. Pushing the thoughts away, he climbed out of the car then headed to the back of the vehicle and opened the trunk. He grabbed his duffel bag and the carry-on filled with all of his necessities: laptop, portable printer, and a few other items that he needed on the road away from his home office. He had always traveled light. The less baggage to lug around the better. It was the same with his personal life.

Frowning, he stared at the B&B—the last place he wanted to be. Why his agent had chosen this B&B he wasn't sure. He had told her he wanted a secluded house as usual. But no, Natalie, his stubborn agent, had said he needed something new, something that wouldn't keep him completely alone. Besides that, she'd said in her perky voice, at a B&B, his meals would be made for him daily. She'd made special arrangements with the owner that he would get very special care and attention. He didn't want special care and attention, he'd growled at her, but the stubborn woman had obviously ignored him.

Confounded woman was always thinking about him, always making sure that everything he needed was taken care of. That way, he could keep pumping out the books so the commissions would continue to pump out for her. These days, he was having nasty thoughts that this was more for her benefit and the publisher's benefit than for him or his fans. Nash felt as if he were a machine that was expected to keep the conveyor belt full at all times with books his readers came to expect, the books that made everybody money…

Dissatisfaction weighed on him.

And then, he'd lost the only person he'd ever cared about…and the words had just dried up.

He'd begun to wonder whether he still had it. He'd begun to wonder whether there was more to life than what he was feeling.

He needed more to his life.

The thought toyed with him.

But what he was pretty certain he didn't need was

someone at the B&B bothering him while he was trying to work. He didn't do hovering, coddling, or smothering. He didn't need someone constantly knocking on his door, interrupting his flow—if he were able to find that while he was here.

Nash Bond worked in solitude. Always had. He liked to choose when he saw people and when he didn't see people. If he wanted to hole up alone, he did. If he wanted to walk the streets and think, he walked the streets and thought. If he wanted to walk the beach and think, he walked the beach and thought. He did not want to have to walk down the stairs, walk past whoever the B&B owner was, make excuses for why he didn't want her breakfast, lunch, or dinner or nosing around, wondering why he was coming or going. He did not like that.

So, he had told Natalie not to book this.

She had booked it anyway.

Her exact words had been, "Nash, you're a grouch and not getting your work done. Too many blank pages lately. You need something to switch things up. Try this," she'd said. "You may love it. What do you have to lose?" He could hear her voice as if she stood beside him, staring at the house.

A seagull flew overhead and poop fell from the sky, barely missing him.

A sign to move. She was right; he'd been having a lot of blank pages.

Fine.

He let out a frustrated breath and stormed forward. He would approach this B&B with the attitude that he would stay here but he would do it his way. If he had to do it, he would do it. He would walk in there and deal with this new situation and make the most of it.

Besides, everything he had known for his entire career was not working right now. Hadn't been working for a year and everyone was waiting on the book that had stalled. Maybe shaking things up would help.

The B&B was pretty, he had to admit. Three stories of bright-yellow wood, white trim, and a bright-red door with a brass door knocker. Colorful flowerpots and flowers everywhere. There were even those little flag things in the flower beds that proclaimed "Welcome!" with little birds on them. Probably had the same thing in his bedroom. Little pillows with happy sayings on them, birds and butterflies, or roses. Yeah, he would undoubtedly be stuck in a rose-wallpapered room with fluffy pink bedspreads and pillows everywhere. *Pillows.*

He hated pillows. He hated flowers. He was a man. He was a man who dove out of airplanes, climbed mountains, dived with sharks. He did not stay in rooms with pillows, roses, and fluff. He liked clean lines. Natalie was going to pay for this.

Nash stalked up the steps, across the wide porch, and banged the brass knocker. Maybe a little too hard as the sound seemed to reverberate in the quiet afternoon. Seconds later, the door flew open and his heart stopped.

The tall blonde—very blonde—with big, huge, blue eyes and pink lips stared at him from just inside the threshold. *Stunning.*

"Hello." She blinked. "I'm sorry." She glanced

back down the hall. "You must be, um." She shook her head just slightly and closed her eyes, seemingly to gather her thoughts.

Was she as startled and stunned as he was? "I'm Nash Bond, your boarder."

"Yes, yes, I…um…sorry. I was working with an overflowing kitchen disaster that I have going on at the moment. Come in. Please. Come in. Excuse me, I have water to turn off. I'll be right back, honestly. Just come in and set your things down. I'm really sorry. Give me a few minutes. I'll be right back. I'm normally…not this way. I promise. Um… I'll give you your key in a minute…uh…just make yourself comfortable and I'll be right back," she rambled, doing a start-stop dance before she spun and headed down the hall away from him.

Only then did he realize that she was partly soaking wet. He had been so stunned by everything; he hadn't even realized her clothing, her top especially, was completely soaked and the edges of her hair were soaked. Portions of her pants too. It looked as if she had been sprayed because some strands of her hair were wet but portions of it weren't. He had been more focused on her face—her eyes, those lips—than the rest of her.

He watched her go and only then did he realize that she had said she had a water disaster.

Setting his things down, he followed her, not particularly happy about the situation but she seemed really flustered. And he heard a hissing noise coming from the room she'd disappeared into and that did not sound good.

Nash raced down the hallway, not certain what he would find. He found pretty much what he'd suspected. "Do you need help?"

She was fumbling with a tool belt that was full of tools. It lay on a kitchen island and she was searching for something as water spewed from under the kitchen sink behind her. The floor, everything, was wet and he realized it was going to be a disaster if it wasn't stopped quickly. These hardwoods needed to be dried immediately.

She looked frantic.

Taking matters into his own hands, he moved past her and into the path of the spewing water.

Erin watched, mortified, as Nash Bond—*the* Nash Bond—got down on the floor in his beautiful dress slacks, that had to be over-the-top expensive, and then moved into the path of the water. Instantly, his white dress shirt was soaked as the water hit him full force before he flipped to his back and crammed his broad shoulders into the open doors of the lower cabinet.

She gasped. This was a disaster.

The man, she knew, wasn't used to doing this kind of thing. He was, after all, one of the best-selling intrigue authors of all time, here to hide out or hole up in her B&B. She had her orders from his agent, publicist, and everyone around him: He was a very grouchy man when writing and he often liked to hole up when working. He often did not eat when the words were flowing. And it was her job to make sure he was fed, that he was comfortable, and that whatever he needed would be taken care of.

He was not here to help her clean up a water disaster.

Erin could not afford for this to go bad.

Despite the fact that she had to get the hardwood dried as quickly as possible or she would sustain costly water damage that she could not afford, she tried again. "Please. I can do this."

"Hardly," he snapped.

Feeling helpless, she could only stare down at the man now on his back with his head and shoulders inside the kitchen cabinet and his long legs sprawled out on the still soaking wet floor.

"Please, Mr. Bond, come out of there. I'll call a plumber." This was not going well at all.

"Do you have a wrench? A wrench, please? I need a wrench." His words were practically barked and she rushed forward to obey him and give him whatever he needed considering he was obviously not going to obey her.

Frantically, she stared at all the different tools. Finally, her eyes landed on the wrench. She grabbed it, bent down and rammed it toward him, too hard. She missed his outstretched hand and hit him in the shoulder.

He grunted.

She cringed. "Sorry."

"Thanks," he growled.

She felt terrible as water sprayed him in the face and covered him as he tried to get the cut-off valve to close. It was hitting her too but she didn't care about herself. The man was drenched and all she could think was that now she would never get the five-star review she'd been praying for from him before he left at the end of his stay.

Moments later, the water stopped and he crawled out from underneath the sink, drenched and scowling.

Despite the dark scowl, she could not help noticing how handsome he was, even soaked all over. His dark hair was plastered to his head and as she looked at him, he swiped a hand through it, slicking it back, and bringing his bold features more clearly into view. The man was not just good-looking; he was striking in a very masculine way.

Unexpected butterflies fluttered in her stomach, startling Erin to action. "Thank you, but really, I wish you hadn't gotten yourself soaked like this."

"It's just water. Do you have towels?"

"Yes." She couldn't think straight, she was so worried about him. But his words spurred her to her feet and she rushed to the laundry room and gathered an armload of folded towels. Hurrying back to the room, she stopped when she saw him standing in the middle of her kitchen, his shirt and pants plastered to him. She gulped at the sight of him. The man was in shape. Then again, she'd read about his adventurous lifestyle, and realized she shouldn't be surprised.

He was still frowning as his gaze met hers, and she felt an electric jolt, as if there were a live electrical wire in the water with them. She moved forward, trying to ignore the awareness flowing through her.

As if he hadn't been affected, and she hoped he hadn't, he grabbed a handful of towels and bent down beside her to start mopping up the water.

"Really, I can take it from here. If you want to go up to your room, it's the only one on the third floor.

There are plenty of towels up there."

"We need to get this cleaned up first. Hopefully, you can call a plumber and get some new pipes installed under there before you're able to use your kitchen again."

"Thank you, I'll call in just a few moments." She gave up protesting, realizing the quicker they got the water cleaned up, the sooner he could go to his room and get dry. They worked in silence and soon the floor was covered with soaking wet towels. She gathered them up, and headed to the laundry room where she dropped them into a basket and grabbed another armload of towels. Her stomach was knotted up as she quickly entered the kitchen where he was waiting.

"Thank you so much." She handed him a fluffy tan towel that he immediately used to scrub his hair and his face and then blotted his upper chest and his arms before wrapping it around his waist. She did the same, needing to get at least the dripping water from her before she led the way across the entrance hall and up the stairs.

"Let me get you to your room where you can get

changed and get out of all that and get comfortable. I promise from here on out everything with your stay will be normal. I'll take care of everything. While you're changing, I'll fix you a platter of snacks. Does that sound good?"

"I'm fine. Just show me to my room. I don't need food. I'll take it from there. You need to get dry too," he said, gruffly.

"Okay, then follow me. I'll come back down, get dry and then bring you up a platter of snacks."

"I don't need any snacks."

She had really messed up and needed to show him how good her hospitality was from here on out. "Oh, you're going to love the muffins that I have for you. They're from this little bakery down the street. They bake them every day. They are fabulous and you're going to fall in love with them while you're here. All my customers fall in love with them, and they'll help you write. I think it's wonderful that you're a writer, and I just want you to know that I'll respect your time, respect your need for quiet. I can fix you whatever you need here in the kitchen."

He scowled. Not exactly a happy camper, it looked like. "I'm fine. I won't need anything."

She studied him for a moment, both of them standing there, dripping wet. She decided that now was not the time to get into the details. "Very well, let me show you to your room."

She led the way up the stairs to the top floor, where he would have the suite all to himself, and hopefully it would be quieter there for him. She did have a few weekend guests coming, but they would be on the second floor at the opposite side of the house from his upstairs room. The room directly below the honeymoon suite was the room she used as a storeroom for cleaning supplies, the vacuum cleaner, clean linens. It helped give the third-floor suite more privacy. She had decided when doing the bed-and-breakfast that she would not have a B&B that had kids because she was marketing it as a romantic getaway or a relaxing adult only getaway. It was better to have a niche. However, when Nash's agent had called requesting to rent the top floor, it was a deal she could not refuse and so her honeymoon suite became a writing retreat for the time being.

She hoped he didn't mind the pillows and the romance of the room. But, it was her biggest room, it was her quietest room, and it had a wonderful view of the water and the town and this was the reason it had specifically been requested by his agent for his extended stay. She was still in the process of getting her B&B renovated, so she could use a long-term resident at the moment since all of her rooms were not being filled for now. And the renovation was costing more than anticipated. The water leak below a good example for why her budget was being strained.

Once they reached the top floor, she opened the door, stepped in, and watched as he entered. He stopped just inside the door beside her and stared.

It was a lovely room; it really, really was. She loved it. It was done in whites with a few pale-pink highlights. She didn't go too over-the-top crazy with pink, but for a man who did not look like fluff or pink would be his cup of tea a little could be too much. And then there were the gold highlights and the white pillows with a few different trims. Pinks and reds were her favorites. She had almost put a floral rose design on one of the walls but had decided that she wanted the B&B to be a little bit more non-traditional and had opted for more clean lines than frilly, rose-covered walls. There was a small deck outside the French doors just big enough for a wrought-iron table and chairs, and she hoped that might be a good place for him to write. The view was spectacular. She thought the room would fit his needs very well. The king-size bed was huge—a gorgeous four-poster frame adorned with a beautiful bedspread of white edged in soft pink. Very romantic.

Standing there with the not-so-happy-looking man, she hoped he wouldn't think it was too frilly for him.

He was a big, very masculine man. She had never actually pictured a single man being in this room. Suddenly, she looked at it through different eyes and began to worry. She decided she might have to make some changes if this wasn't always going to be used as a honeymoon suite.

"I hope it's okay?" She heard the uncertainty in her voice.

"It will be fine." After hesitating, he stepped into the room and then turned and nodded.

He looked as if he held back on saying something else, and she couldn't help but wonder what that might be. Honestly, it didn't look like it was good.

"Very well. I'll be downstairs. Just take your time and let me know if I can get you anything else. I'll check you in. No need to come down and do that. All is well."

He nodded and didn't say anything else. She backed up and closed the door. Feeling a little bit awkward, she just stood there and stared at it. The man was a little intense. Not exactly her happy-to-be-here weekender she had been used to. Obviously, she was going to have to adjust to that attitude. The agent hadn't been kidding when she said that he was usually a little bit of a grouch. Then again, what could she expect after what she'd just put him through?

Oh, how she needed this to go well. A five-star review from Nash Bond could do wonders for her fledgling business, and now she had her work cut out for her after the disastrous way his stay had begun.

This was a make-it-or-break-it situation and she truly had to fight to keep her chin up and positive thoughts flowing. Because Nash Bond did not look at all happy about being here.

CHAPTER TWO

Turning away from the door, Erin hurried down the stairs, her mind rolling as she went through different ways to put a smile on the man's face. Yes, so they said he was normally a grump when he was writing, but this was her place, and she wasn't used to that and felt it was her duty to put a smile on his face. She wanted the people who were here at her bed-and-breakfast to be happy. So, she was quite certain that she could come up with a way of making him happy. She had to! A B&B survived by good reviews and happy customers. The last thing she needed was Nash putting up a bad review. She was really obsessing over this, but she couldn't seem to stop.

Though, the more she thought about it, the more she believed the man would probably not bother with putting up any kind of review, good or bad. But, if by chance he did put up a review, she wanted it to be five stars all the way. A five-star review from a famous author could do wonders for her business.

Once downstairs, Erin called the plumber and he assured her he would be there within the hour, which was a relief. Then she called her sister-in-law, Rosie, and explained what had happened.

"Is he there?" Rosie asked, excitement bringing her voice up a notch. "I looked him up and good heavens, the man is something. Don't you think?"

"Yes, he's here, and it was a disaster. He came in right in the middle of the water busting out of the cabinet and he got down into the cabinet and turned the water off while getting soaked to the bone. It's so embarrassing. The whole place is a mess. As soon as we get off the phone, I'm going to have to mop the floors again to get every drop of water up before things get ruined."

"I'm so sorry. But thankfully he was there to get the water turned off."

"It was just terrible and, I mean, I haven't had anything like this happen before. I wasn't expecting to have a plumbing problem. I didn't even realize there *was* a plumbing problem! This old house is going to have several, I'm sure, but this was just so unexpected. And he had no business having to fix my problems."

"Don't worry, it'll be fine." Rosie was always upbeat. "You didn't answer me. Is he as gorgeous as his picture, do you think?"

"Yes, Rosie, he is handsome."

"Oh, I knew it. Is he charming?"

Charming was not the word she would use. "We were so busy cleaning up that I don't know about his charm. But you're right, it's going to be fine. I'm just tied up right now. I just don't need this to be a bad experience."

"Honestly, Erin, your B&B is beautiful. You do such a great job and you're very hospitable. Plus, you serve the best muffins in town." She laughed, and Erin smiled. The muffins *were* the best in town and Rosie baked them at Bake My Day. Everyone in town was now addicted to Rosie's muffins, as were Erin's customers.

"Yes, I do, and on that note, I want you to know that I'm going to have to postpone getting together with you and Lulu. Maybe we can do it tomorrow or a couple of days down the road. I'm not giving up on getting Lulu and Brad to set their wedding date. But right now, I need to mop this mess up, get it looking decent, wait for the plumber, and I'm going to take him some of your muffins. That will make his day and put a smile on his face."

She was smiling when she hung up. She had a plan.

Nash came out of the bathroom in clean jeans and a comfortable polo-shirt, put his hands on his hips, and stared at the room. Thankfully, it wasn't as bad as it could have been. It was white—very white—with hints of pink and red, very fluffy, but there were no flowers all over the room and he was thankful for that. There were pillows, a lot of pillows, but he could put them in the corner and ignore them. The rest of the room was pretty tastefully done. There were no little dainty chairs; instead, the chair and couch in the corner of the large room were both comfortable looking and would fit his big frame if he wanted to work there. The desk was not a little tiny girly desk either; it was a big, fairly decent-sized desk that would fit him for his writing and his printer and his computer. There was a surprise, though, totally unexpected—French doors leading out to a small balcony. He moved across the room and opened the doors, swinging them wide as he walked out into the open space and stopped, staring out across the rooftops to the ocean, glistening a brilliant blue topaz with white clouds hovering overhead, fluffier than the pillows inside his room. It was magnificent. This was why Natalie had chosen this B&B, nosey as she was, wanting him to have something different. She'd still given him a view. A place he could sit and contemplate. A space to write.

He still wasn't happy that she'd gone against his

wishes for solitude but at least this small space made up for some of his disappointment in her choice. It wasn't very big, but it was big enough for him to sit and enjoy the view of the water. It was very private. He walked to the edge of the balcony and looked down at the small garden two floors below. It appeared to be a secret garden, small and flanked by tall foliage. He seemed to have it all to himself. Tropical flowers bordered the trees and shrubs that blocked out the homes on the side of the house but didn't interfere with the view of the ocean, which was at a different angle toward the front of the house. He could see the bay in all of its glory. It was in the distance, overlooking a neighborhood that was between him and the beach, only a quick walk away. He could see the marina, where there were several boats—sailboats, fishing boats, all different kinds of boats. The blue topaz water was amazing and the sun glinting off it was a very calming, pretty picture. Yes, he could write here.

Hopefully, he could write. He needed to be able to write. Needed to shake off the clouds that hovered over his creativity, hindering his work. Barring the words from flowing. He inhaled and let his gaze sweep the landscape, the garden, and the room. He hoped, here in this place, the words would come.

If it remained as quiet as it was now and he wasn't constantly being bothered, maybe the words would flow.

This was a small town, and he didn't know whether there were any places that stayed open late as his days were not the same as others. When the words were flowing he didn't stop the flow by interrupting his muse with lunch or dinner, he kept going. Which meant that sometimes, most times, his days and nights were mixed up. He had a thing for coffee shops, and late-night diners when there was hardly anybody in them. Did this town have that? Natalie really tried to shake things up for him this time, so she might not have taken that into consideration. Especially considering she'd put him in this B&B. Resentment that his wishes had been ignored set in. He shook it off because truth was, he needed things to be shaken up.

He really needed to get this book done.

A knock sounded at his door. Spinning, he

scowled. He'd only been here less than thirty minutes, and already, they were knocking on his door. Striding across the room, he yanked the door open a little harder than he had planned. He knew this when Erin jumped and the tray she had in her hands shook. For a moment, he thought she might drop it, but she got control of it.

"I brought you some muffins, just like I promised," she said in a cheery voice, smiling brightly at him.

She had obviously scrubbed her own hair down and changed quickly into a bright-pink T-shirt/blouse thing and white jeans. His eyes scanned down the tray of muffins and cookies, a little pot that he wasn't sure what it had in it, a glass of what looked like water with lemon in a little bottle beside it, and little things of cream and sugar. But, his scan went past there, to her feet with bright-pink toe polish. He swept his gaze back up to meet her eyes, eyes as blue as the topaz water outside his window. He was struck by her beauty—those blue eyes, small nose, and pale-pink lips that spread into an engaging, wide smile. Now that her hair was dry, it was silky blonde, thick and hanging straight down her back. His hands suddenly itched to touch it and see whether it was as silky as it looked.

He didn't need to encourage her interruptions, he reminded himself, and frowned. If she started interrupting now, she would the entire time. He needed to set the rules now. "I really don't need anything."

"Nonsense," she said briskly, her voice light. "You haven't tried these muffins or pastries. They are fabulous, and the coffee also comes from Bake My Day." She'd slipped past him, as he hadn't completely blocked the door, and as she flounced into the room, the scent of something sweet engulfed him. It was an amazing scent of the orange and cinnamon wafting from the tray as she passed. Unable to stop, he left the door open and followed her as she carried the tray to a small table beside the French doors. He wasn't sure if he was smelling the muffins or her but he was drawn to her or the scent the muffins or both.

She set the tray down and then turned. He had stopped closer to her than intended and now stood a little nearer than was probably appropriate. But the scents were far too enticing. And now as she looked at him, so close, her eyes widened at his nearness. He noted that she came up to about his eyebrows. She was tall, but he was taller. It hit him instantly that she was the perfect height for him to kiss.

The thought jumped out at him.

Why should he be thinking things like that about his innkeeper?

He wasn't here for anything like that. He was here to write.

"I hope the room is good. I know you're going to like the muffins. I also brought you coffee. I wasn't sure if you liked coffee, but I figured you probably did, and if you don't, I brought you some lemon water. I have tea, hot tea—I could do that for you instead. Or some iced sweet tea. I could do you some lemonade if you preferred. I have all kinds of things downstairs. Just let me know what you like and I can get that for you every day." She spoke swiftly, as if afraid to let him interject a response. Or because she was nervous.

"I'm a coffee drinker but I can take care of that myself. I'll get my own machine for my room."

Confusion slackened her expression but she recovered quickly. "There's no need for that. I keep a pot warming downstairs and I can bring it up to your room or you are welcome to come down and grab a cup anytime. I know that you're here to write, and I don't want to get in your way. I just want to feed you like your agent, Natalie, has asked me to and to see to anything else you might need, such as coffee and fresh snacks during the day or night. I'm thrilled you're here and I know that you are going to be able to write a wonderful book while visiting Sunset Bay."

He tried to move the scowl that was on his face; he could feel it, but it was stuck there. He couldn't let this woman get the impression that he liked intrusion despite the fact that he couldn't seem to stop looking at her. "Thank you, but I won't need you to bring me anything. I'm quite capable of taking care of myself. I will take you up on getting the coffee when I want it and then I can go out and get anything else I need."

"But—"

"I'll keep water in the..." He looked around. "There is a small refrigerator, isn't there?"

"No, but you're welcome to keep whatever you want in the refrigerator downstairs. Although, like I said, I have all of that there already, no real need for you to buy your own. Natalie has made arrangements for you to have anything you need out of my kitchen— anything. All you have to do is just let me know. Or, I mean, you're welcome to come down at night and find something to eat. There's always something in there, I promise you. Or if it's not what you want, I'd be happy to pick it up for you or to make if it's something homemade you'd like."

"Natalie makes too many plans. I'll be fine." The words were blunt.

Her brows knit together, and he could see her mind whirling behind the blue. He almost felt bad.

She waved her pretty pink-tipped fingered hand at the tray. "Well, I guess, I'll leave this here, but…I promise, you're going to love them." She tilted her head to the side and her eyes searched his. He remained impassive, holding his ground. Her shoulders slumped slightly. "Very well, I guess I'll leave you alone." She turned to leave but immediately turned back to him. "I serve afternoon treats and snacks and a little wine in the den around six, and you're welcome to come join us and have that, and you can bring it up to your room if you'd like, or I can bring it to you." Her brows knit. "Whatever you'd like."

She was persistent and obviously hard of hearing. He hitched a brow and remained silent, determined not to repeat himself again.

She nodded, gave a hesitant smile, and then, as if forcing herself, she gave him a bright smile. "Okay then, I'll see you later." Then she headed toward the door and was gone.

The door closed behind her and he stood there like a stone, staring at the door and feeling like a complete oaf.

But, no time to think about that. It was time to sit down and see if words would come and if not, then time to make them come. Ignoring the muffins, he picked up the coffee, grabbed his laptop from the desk, and walked out onto the balcony.

CHAPTER THREE

The arrogant man had not left his room all afternoon. Erin stood in the kitchen with her arms crossed, her fingers tapping on her side, trying to figure out what to do. Clearly, he was not happy with her earlier, as she had left him standing there with a tray of muffins and coffee and a scowl on his face. He was odd and hard to get along with, just as she'd feared.

What to do?

Maybe he didn't even eat muffins? He hadn't been happy that she'd brought him the snack and that had been obvious. This Natalie, this agent of his, who had said it was going to be Erin's responsibility to feed him while he was here and to put up with his grumpiness, hadn't warned her that the man literally didn't want her in the vicinity of anything to do with him. How was she supposed to be hospitable when the man did not want hospitality?

She was left with a dilemma. She'd been paid extra money to feed him and she wouldn't take money and not do her job. But he had *glowered* at her—yes, that was much more appropriate a word than scowled. She was suddenly reminded of *Beauty and the Beast*. Not that she was a beauty, but, well, you know, Belle had to go face that beast and so did she, it seemed. She was, after all, the host of the B&B, and he was a guest—a very well-paying guest. She had to pull up her big girl panties and do this. She had to and she would do this.

All her other guests had come down for the hospitality hour. They'd had wine. They'd had coffee. They'd had muffins and quiche and her homemade chicken salad that was to die for, if she did say so herself. They'd loved the little hand sandwiches on flaky croissants. He'd missed out, holed up there, hopefully writing. If that were the case, she wished him well but still, the man had to eat.

She made him a nice tray after everyone had gone their separate ways and she'd given him ample time to come down and join in. She set the sandwiches on a colorful plate with chips on the side and a fruit cup, along with fresh baked lemon cookies. She added a sprig of rosemary and a daisy in a small shot glass-size vase just to add another touch. Everything was delicious and looked great.

Would he think the sandwiches were silly? The broad-shouldered, serious man…eating a croissant didn't actually fit. But, tonight that was what she had to offer. She would do better tomorrow.

Picking up the tray, she told herself she could do this. She could walk up those stairs like the very generous and lovely host that she was and deliver this tray without shaking, without cringing when he opened the door. And without ogling him.

Moments later, she walked up the long, suddenly

endless three flights of stairs, and when she reached his room, she took a deep breath and then knocked on the door.

"Who's there," he practically growled. Though muffled through the door, it was most certainly a growl.

Arrogant man. He knew very well who was knocking on his door. *Who else would it be?*

She bit her lip and forced her temper down. "It's Erin. I brought you your dinner, or at least, something to nourish you."

Silence.

She waited there, holding the tray, hoping that the ice in the lemonade wouldn't melt before he opened the door. At last, the door opened, and a very gorgeous, very unhappy man stood there, his dark eyes drilling into her with impatience.

"I told you I didn't want anything."

She did not like his attitude. "And I've been paid to feed you." She tossed her hair slightly, a bad habit that she had when she was nervous. "Here's your dinner. If this isn't enough, there are some nice restaurants in town if you'd prefer to go out for something. But, I thought since you haven't left your room since you arrived that you might be deep in thought or writing and need a little something."

Like earlier, he didn't move out of her way or invite her in, so she swept past him, feeling his eyes on her. She got a whiff of his aftershave, a subtle spicy scent that tickled her senses. She tried to ignore the enticing scent and focused on the table, where she'd left the muffins earlier. Sure enough, not a single muffin appeared to have been eaten. The water glass was empty and the coffee mug was missing, so she assumed he'd enjoyed that at least.

"Well, I'm glad I showed up since you didn't eat anything. How you resisted those muffins I'll never know. You're really missing out because Rosie down at Bake My Day makes muffins into an art form."

"Yes, you've already told me she makes delicious muffins. I was in the middle of writing something when you knocked on the door."

She understood that this was code for, "You broke my train of thought and interrupted me and I'm not happy about it." She frowned, perplexed at how to handle him. "I'm sorry that I did that. I know you're here to write. I'll just set this here on the table and I'll take the muffins away. I'm sure someone here at the B&B will love them," she said, barely controlling her irritation as she picked the tray up and turned. He stood in her way, staring at her with his thick brows dipping together over those dark eyes. An unexpected shiver raced through her as they stared at each other and took the bite out of her irritation. "I-I'll leave you alone now," she said, her voice strained. She marched toward the door, needing space between them.

"Erin," he said from behind her, in a voice a combination of irritation and maybe remorse.

Maybe.

She stopped, but didn't turn around right away. Her stomach felt weak as she slowly turned to look at him.

"Look." He raked a hand through thick, dark hair and huffed out a breath. "I'm here to write. I need my space. I am a fully-grown man, if you haven't noticed—"

Oh, despite not wanting to, she had definitely noticed.

"—and I know that Natalie, my agent, has specifically told you to feed me and take care of me and coddle me like a child. The reality is, she thinks that is part of her job. But it's not. If I wanted someone to tell me how to eat, I would have married someone a long time ago. And as you can see, I'm not married. This isn't your fault, and I know that you're probably hating me at the moment, but I just need to write."

She cleared her dry throat. "I understand. However, Natalie paid me extra to take care of you. It's not in my nature to take money and then not deliver. So that leaves me kind of in a dilemma. I can give you back the money and I can leave you alone. But really, what are you going to eat if you're busy writing like you were today? I'm a very good cook and surely there is some kind of agreement we could come to that would suit your needs. Rosie's muffins are wonderful, but if you prefer something else, I'll make it for you. If you prefer eggs and bacon, I'll make you eggs and bacon. If you would prefer quiche…you probably don't eat quiche, I'm sorry… I'll make you anything you want. Just look at it like you're staying at a hotel and you can have room service when you want it. And when I'm not here, because I do take a few hours off at times, I can leave the food in the refrigerator for you. Or, if you'd prefer to raid the refrigerator instead of me bringing it up, I'll just make things and leave it there for you to get when you feel like it. I just hate the idea of you being hungry."

"I don't want the money back. Let's make a deal. If I get hungry, I'll come downstairs and raid your refrigerator. If I'm not hungry, I won't come downstairs. How's that?" He crossed his arms and cocked his head, looking at her from beneath those brows, reminding her of a pirate.

Her lip twitched as she fought not to smile. The man was perfectly capable of taking care of himself. "Fine. I think that we have come to an agreement."

She let out a long sigh, and then she saw a

miracle, yes, a miracle…*the* Nash Bond smiled.

And her knees went weak.

Nash watched Erin go and when the door closed behind her, he laughed. The blamed woman had been persistent and she'd been in a predicament. Natalie's fault. But she was right. He was going to get hungry and if he were staying at a hotel, like he sometimes liked to do, he would have just called room service when he felt like calling room service. Or, he would have gone downstairs and gotten something in the bar or restaurant.

They had an agreement now that might work for him because though he didn't want interruptions, he did like this room. When she'd knocked on his door and interrupted him, his fingers had been flying across the keyboard, which, sadly, hadn't happened in a long time. Words had been hard to come by all year and it had been exhilarating to finally be writing again. When she had tapped on his door, the interruption had made him snappish. He frowned. He couldn't spend the whole time he was here making her upset when she'd only been doing what she'd agreed to do. It was easy to see she was the type of person who would take special care of the people staying at her establishment. He had to admit he'd liked watching her smile. Liked the sweet pink that had touched her cheeks when he'd stared at her too long. He'd kept thinking about when he'd first arrived and she'd flung the front door open and she'd been standing there in front of him. She had taken his breath away.

He didn't want his breath taken away; he was here to write a book. A book that had to be written. He didn't need distractions and his pretty hostess could easily be just that. Walking to the balcony, he leaned against the doorframe and stared across the distance to the topaz water that now glistened with gold as the sun began to set in the distance. It was beautiful. Peaceful. Something called to him as he stood there. Maybe it was the fact that the words had flowed at last from what had felt for too long, like a vise clamping down on his creative mind.

He breathed deeply of the salty air, smelled the sea, and let his mind roam. It had been a little while since he'd spent time at the coast and from where he was, he could actually see a little bit of the town and the people moving around. It did look like a nice, quaint, small place full of character. He saw seagulls and heard their cries. He spotted a large pelican soaring high above the house and then it tilted its wings like a cargo plane and zoomed silently toward his balcony, buzzing him like a fighter jet giving warning. It came so close that Nash straightened from the doorframe he'd been leaning against, afraid for a moment that it was coming straight through the open doors and into the room with him. He was certain that Erin Sinclair would not welcome a large pelican tearing up her honeymoon suite as it banged about and panicking as it tried to find its way back outside again. But, though it had flown quite close to his balcony, it changed course at the last moment and headed back out to sea.

Nash moved to the balcony and watched the big brown bird, awkward to look at but a graceful thing to watch as it flew with purpose over the rooftops toward the water. Its wingspan was very large and its feet hanging down below it were not small either. He'd probably been as close up as he'd ever been to a pelican in those moments he'd thought his room was about to be invaded. He smiled, wondering whether this was the last he'd see of the bold pelican. And he wondered what else he might see from this balcony with a view.

Again, it hit him that this was a good place to write. He picked up the glass of water that was almost empty and sat down in the chair beside the small table where his computer waited. Pushing everything out of his mind, he stared at the last words he had written. Then he put his fingers on the keyboard and began typing.

The words that had been interrupted moments before flowed again.

Yes, Natalie had been right…this was a place he

could write.

And with luck, maybe in the writing he could find the joy he'd lost a year ago when he'd lost his footing, lost the only person who'd ever really known him. The one who'd saved him and set him on the path of purpose instead of destruction.

It was probably too much to hope for, but still he hoped for it.

But for now, he let the words come and he typed as fast as the wind, not wanting to lose any of them, as he knew more these days than ever before, that every word that came to him was precious.

CHAPTER FOUR

S ometime in the wee hours of the morning, long after he'd closed the French doors and moved to the writing desk and continued getting the bones of the story pounded out until at last, he couldn't see straight, he fell into bed, feeling good about the story.

He woke wanting coffee and his computer. He hadn't felt this way in so long he didn't want the magic to stop. Pulling on his jeans and a shirt, he pushed his hair off his forehead and quietly opened the door and slipped out onto the landing. The house was silent. He peered over the banister that was a clear shot to the first floor. There was no movement. Moving silently down the stairs on his bare feet, he was relieved there was no one around. It was nearly ten o'clock, so maybe he'd caught everyone gone. He found a pot of coffee warming in the dining area with an array of different size cups. Visitor's choice, he assumed. He picked the largest mug in the rack and set it beside the coffeepot.

There was a fancy glass cake holder or whatever they called it with a cinnamon swirled pound cake sliced thick and ready inside. There was a covered warming pan, too, and he lifted the lid to find several fluffy biscuits filled with bacon, eggs, and cheese. His stomach rumbled as he picked one up, and placed it on a blue ceramic plate. He passed up the cake as he reached for the large brown mug he'd set there, filled it with steaming coffee and breathed in the scent of it. *Bless whoever first discovered coffee.* He took a cautionary drink and the moment the strong brew touched his lips then burned down his throat, he started to feel the dregs of his late-night and the cobwebs clearing. Life was good.

Taking his bounty, he moved toward the doorway. He paused, glanced around for Erin, surprised she hadn't popped out from behind a door and tried to force muffins on him. Not seeing her, he headed back upstairs. He needed a shower and then he would be ready to dive back into the story. But first he went to the French doors. He set the plate on the table beside them before he pulled them open and let the mid-morning sunshine and fresh air inside. He sipped his coffee, picked up his breakfast sandwich, and walked out onto the balcony to take in the view. He'd have to tell Natalie she'd had good instincts because his story was coming along and it was good. This place inspired him.

He set his coffee on the table then went back in and got his computer. He'd shower later; the itch to write was too strong. He settled into his chair, and as his computer came on, he took a bite of his sandwich. It was delicious. Within moments, he was typing again.

A sound below him drew him out of his story as it caught his attention…humming.

He didn't have to stand up to look over the back

edge of the balcony because he was sitting with his back to it. He leaned back and glanced down. The second story room didn't have a balcony so he had a straight shot below. He spotted Erin. Her blonde hair sparkled in the morning sunlight as she moved around the lawn, watering the flowers and humming softly. He couldn't really make out what it was; he just knew she was humming something very quietly. She seemed content and he watched her, enjoying how at peace she seemed. Then, feeling intrusive, he turned back to his story. Her humming grew closer as she moved below him. Propping his elbow on the table, he ran his fingers through his hair and grasped his forehead as he sat there and let out a small, silent groan. *How could he concentrate with her below him, humming like that?*

Maybe she only came out there at certain times of the day and hummed. Though very enjoyable, it distracted him. Hopefully, she wouldn't be there all the time. He liked this spot. He liked this spot a lot. He stood and moved back inside with his computer. It was a nice desk. It was a nice room. He liked the balcony better.

He liked her humming but didn't want to listen to it while he was trying to concentrate. Her humming messed up his concentration. He'd written a good amount of words in the short time he'd been writing; he'd been on another roll. Which was a good thing and he didn't want interruptions while they were flowing. There would be plenty of days they wouldn't come so easily. Those days, he needed to let the story…simmer and long walks on the beach were good for that. Hikes on trails were good for him. He wondered, suddenly, whether Erin Sinclair liked walking on the beach or hiking. The moment the thought entered his head, he knew he was in trouble. If he didn't get her out of his mind, he was going to mess up his writing. He needed this book in more ways than just to satisfy his agent, his publisher, and his fans. He needed it for himself, to know that he could still write.

He needed to know that he still had what it took to put words to paper. He'd lost that when his dad died. He wasn't sure whether everyone was affected by their father's death like he was, but it had been as if when his dad had left this world, he'd taken with him Nash's ability to create words. His dad had been his inspiration. His dad had been his best friend. His dad had been the rock that had steered him through his wild childhood, his rough years. His dad had been the man who rescued him when he was desperate and alone.

Like an adventure hero, his dad had swept in, scooped him up, and made him his. And then he'd made him into the man he was today. But long before his time, Gerald Bond had been taken from Nash. At the age of sixty-two—still young, still vibrant—his dad had dropped dead in an instant. He had been the striking image of a healthy man and a weak valve in his heart had dropped him like a rock. And in doing so, Nash also had dropped.

True enough—Nash's heart still beat in his chest, but he was *not* the same. And he had not been able to write a word since.

That wasn't true… He'd written words, but they didn't have the same spark, the same energy. They had been worthless and Nash deleted them. Until yesterday, he hadn't written any words worth keeping.

Now, staring at the computer screen, he thought these were words he could keep. And to that, he wasn't sure who he owed the compliment. He was glad to be writing again, but his heart still ached with the loss of his dad.

Enough of that. Enough of wallowing in the sorrow that had held him in its grip for little over a year. He stood and with the soft, gentle humming calling him back toward the balcony, he knew it was time to check out the beach. Past time. It was not time to hang his head over the balcony and ask his landlady what the song was that she was humming.

He needed a distraction from her. Closing his computer, he grabbed his phone and his shades, and he left the room.

"I'm so glad we were finally able to get together this afternoon." Rosie smiled at Erin and Lulu across the small metal café table that she had recently set along the sidewalk outside her bakery.

Customers were loving her new chairs and her

new tables. It was a little crowded on the sidewalk, but she'd had room to place seven of the small tables against the wall of her bakery, still allowing for people to move along the sidewalk. And now, she sat there with Erin and Lulu, about to enjoy some time together.

"Me too." Erin practically groaned then took a sip of her caramel mocha coffee, closing her eyes and savoring the taste. "I needed a break and this."

Lulu met Rosie's gaze and then they both studied Erin. She'd been tense when she'd arrived and had Rosie asking whether something was wrong. Erin had quickly—too quickly—denied it, though. But she'd made her a sweet caramel mocha with extra sugar and she'd taken it almost greedily when Rosie had handed it to her just now. It was plain to see that Erin had something on her mind and Rosie wondered whether it was what she suspected. "How is your new guest?" she asked. Erin had told her family and close friends that Nash Bond had rented a room for a couple of months and Rosie couldn't help her curiosity. The man was really handsome and he was single.

"Yes, how is he?" Lulu echoed her, excitement in her question.

"He's very maddening." Erin frowned.

"*Really?* Is he as hard to deal with as I read he could be?" Rosie had read he was elusive and could be hard to get along with when he was in the middle of a book. But she figured if he was creating and concentrating, that being interrupted might be hard on him. She'd read that some authors were like that. A lot of them.

"He's dreamy in his pictures, don't you think, Erin? Is he as gorgeous as he looks in photos?" Lulu asked, eyeing Erin like Rosie was as they searched for any sign that Erin found him attractive. "Of course, he's not as dreamy as my Brad!" Lulu held her coffee with both hands, her eyes bright over the top of the cup before she took a drink.

Rosie loved Lulu, with her hair the color of fire and her tender heart. She and Lulu had both been blessed to be loved by a Sinclair, her by Adam and Lulu by Brad. Both of them were as handsome as men could be but it was their hearts that she and Lulu had fallen for. She desperately loved Adam, and Lulu was madly in love with Brad. Rosie wanted that for Erin and also for her sister Cassie. Both the Sinclair sisters were devoted to their work, which was fine and she knew could be fulfilling. But still, Rosie wanted more for them. And though she hadn't said anything when she'd looked at the photo of Nash Bond, she'd had a hope that maybe his trip was fate—destiny—as her own move to Sunset Bay had been and also Lulu's. For both of them, if they hadn't come to this romantic seaside town, they wouldn't have met their men.

As she'd stared at the strong, serious-eyed, and dark features of the famous author, she'd wondered…could destiny be happening again? She hoped so, but she'd keep that hope to herself. Erin wasn't a person to push. She'd let Lulu do the pushing and the questioning, and Rosie would do the listening. And if there was any confiding to be done by Erin, she hoped her sister-in-law would confide in her and that she'd be able to help her in any way that she could.

She wanted the best for her. But she was jumping the gun on this…the man had just arrived, for heaven's sake. What was she thinking?

Erin let her frustrations ease as she sipped her delicious mocha coffee and studied Rosie and Lulu as thoughts of just how handsome and pleasing to look at Nash was. Of course, Lulu believed Brad was the most handsome man in the world and Erin couldn't help but smile about that. Lulu was a dog lover and owned a dog walking service and newly opened doggy daycare, so she was used to smelly when wet. This thought made Erin laugh as she thought of Nash drenched two days ago when he'd arrived. He hadn't been smelly though. Erin had always teased her brothers about being smelly creatures when they'd come in after playing football or some other sport that they'd done growing up. She pushed the childhood thoughts away. She was just happy Lulu and her brother loved each other. And, he wasn't the smelly creature she had grown up with anymore. He was the fire chief and local hero and had been one of the most eligible bachelors in town, as were her other brothers. She still teased him that she'd never understand why so many women in town had drooled over the man until he had found his match in Lulu.

And Rosie. Rosie and her brother Adam, the town doctor, were a perfect match. And now, looking at her friends with their expectant and curious expressions, she suddenly wondered when she would be ready to find the kind of love that they'd found with her brothers. Of course, Lulu and Brad hadn't yet set a date and they were all hoping soon. She felt like it would be soon. Hoped it would but that was in their own time. And her falling in love, she assumed, would come in her own time too.

When it did, would she be ready?

She was confused by Nash Bond. The hardnosed man had set a buzz going inside her that was restless and hadn't stopped since he'd arrived. And though she tried, she felt irritated every time she thought of him— which was often. Like now. *Grrrr.* The man had snuck down that morning and gotten a breakfast biscuit and a mug of coffee.

"So, I mean, is he nice?" Rosie asked again, startling her from her wandering thoughts.

"Okay, I'll be honest with you. He's a big grouch is what he is. He doesn't even want me to come around. How am I even supposed to be hospitable to him when he's acting like that? I mean, we finally came to a deal, where he comes down and rummages through the refrigerator where I'll leave him food. But what kind of hospitality is that from me? I'm just not comfortable with it. My reputation is riding on my hospitality and this just feels wrong."

Rosie had a disbelieving look on her face. "Oh, I would hate that too. I mean, my coffee shop is here so that I can treat people and make them smile with my own personal touch. I'm with you. I wouldn't want him fending for himself. And it sounds like he really is as grumpy as the articles that I read said he is. That's disappointing."

Lulu frowned. "But in his picture online he's smiling. I mean, not in all his pictures but most of them. He was in the one where he's hanging off the side of a mountain, and that picture I saw of him skydiving, he was smiling. They reminded me a lot of those pictures you have of Tate, your brother. "

Erin smiled, despite her mood. "Yes, I know Tate is my brother." She had a sudden spark of humor. Rosie giggled and Lulu grinned.

"So you're telling us there isn't any spark between the two of you?" Rosie asked.

Erin took a drink of her warm coffee. "No. The fact that he is like my brother is not a five-star recommendation for me. Those things that make him smile scare me to death. Your muffins make me smile and they didn't make him smile. Oh no, I took him a whole platter of them and the man passed them up. Never ate a single one. Can you believe that? He might be gorgeous but the man and I have nothing in common. Those muffins are irresistible. Your orange marmalade ones, your strawberry cream cheese delight, that cinnamon toasted coconut crunch thing you make—they were sitting there on his desk all afternoon and he didn't touch them. Do you know how amazing his room smelled?"

Her voice was rising but she couldn't help it. "It was unbelievable! I mean, I was being so hospitable. I cannot imagine the fortitude it must have taken to pass them up. I mean, it just shows me that the man has no humor. I mean, if you can't even enjoy one little delight, what kind of humor can you have? He's a grouch. A pure grouch. He's a handsome, adventurous grouch who I have absolutely nothing in common with. So, don't think I don't realize what you two are thinking. Stop. He is definitely not my type." She crossed her arms, feeling hot and flustered.

Lulu and Rosie stared at her, their eyes wide.

"Your type?" A mischievous smile spread on Lulu's face. "We didn't say anything about him being your type. I think you're interested."

"Yes, I hear a hint of excitement in your voice." Rosie looked smug.

Erin groaned. *How had she given herself away?* "You two, come on, I'm not interested. Again, the man is gorgeous, adorable, grumpy, adventurous, and completely, absolutely, not my type. Besides, I'm not looking for a husband. I'm not looking for a boyfriend. I'm opening a B&B and marketing it well. I have no time. So, don't get your hopes up and do not start pushing this guy on me. He is here to write and he has made that absolutely clear. He is here to write a book and that's it. I mean, I have to admit that I did feel a few butterflies when I was around him—okay, I shouldn't admit that to you girls because it isn't helping my case but I mean, honestly, I didn't know I even had butterflies anymore. I thought they all died. So I might not be his type and he isn't my type, but he is sexy and I now know my butterflies are alive and well."

Rosie and Lulu giggled and she knew she'd just messed up. She closed her eyes, bit into her muffin and chewed. It was the best way to keep her mouth shut.

CHAPTER FIVE

It was the second day in a row that Nash had made it out of the B&B without being noticed. He wasn't sure how it had happened, but he had done it. It was a relief. He thought that everyone had checked out of the inn this morning but he wasn't positive. He'd found the breakfast sandwiches again this morning and late in the night, he'd found a well-stocked refrigerator and had eaten until he was stuffed. He did that a lot when the words were coming in crazy fast, and he didn't want to let them stop. Yesterday when he'd walked on the beach, he'd found a small taco stand and grabbed a bite before he'd snuck back into the B&B and up to his room. He'd spotted a couple of people in the parlor of the place but had headed up the stairs before they noticed him and he'd been able to avoid conversation. There had been a pitcher of lemon water on a small stand beside his door and a metal carafe of hot coffee beside a plate of cookies. He'd smiled, despite himself. His hostess hadn't completely given up on supplying him with her hospitality. And he'd picked up the tray and taken it into his room.

That had been his snack through the evening and his late night of writing until he'd gone down to the kitchen. Now, as he walked down the street, he passed several people. None of them seemed to recognize him. And that was a relief. It was nice. He liked not always being recognized. Part of it was that he'd not shaved for a couple of days and his scruffiness helped. The town was quaint and cute, and he'd admitted on yesterday's walk that Natalie did a good job. She had found a great place for him to work and explore and to create.

It was a tourist trap, he could tell that, but in a nice

way. It still had character. There wasn't a seashell shop on every corner, even though the street that he walked down was called "Seashell Lane." He was fast approaching Main Street and the Bake My Day bakery. He'd not come this way yesterday; instead, he'd gone straight down to the beach from the house. His steps slowed as he took in the small bakery on the corner with tables against the wall and colorful awnings that called to people to stop and enjoy. His gaze snagged on three women sitting at one of the tables and he halted in his tracks when he realized one of them was Erin. She sat at the table and as he watched, she laughed at something the red-headed lady said. The sound of her laugh curled in his chest like a warm embrace. Instantly, he backed up behind a bush. Stood there, not sure exactly what to do, but knowing that he did not want to walk down past them and get roped into a conversation that he had no idea where it would go.

He turned and headed back the way he'd come, then turned down the first road that led to the beach and the blue water glistening in the distance. He passed small, colorful houses with brightly colored shutters and small sidewalks. Outside he saw surfboards and fishing equipment, and it was obvious to see that the people here enjoyed the outdoors. He reached the end of the sidewalk, where the concrete met the white sand. First of the week like it was, the beach wasn't terribly crowded, though there were a few kids flying kites, people sitting on towels, people sitting in recliners and watching the water. He had his jogging shoes on, and had changed into his khakis and a soft blue T-shirt for comfort. He strolled out onto the sugar sand. As soft and silky as any he'd ever walked on.

Bending, he scooped up a handful, letting the fine grains sift through his fingers. It was soft all right, mushed beneath the soles of his shoes as he walked out to the water's edge. He thought if he'd get out to the wet part, he would walk and think and get his new scenes lined up and ready. It really felt good to be able to mull over the plot of his book. He started walking, put his hands in his pocket, and walked toward the wind. It wasn't bad and it smelled of sea salt and he thought he could smell caramel corn. He glanced up toward the buildings in the distance that were the strip and he was fairly certain someone up there was making candy corn or caramel corn…something good. It complemented the salt in the air. He paused, looking out at the water, and thought of his dad.

Like a clamp on his heart, the pain was sharp and then the ache remained. He raked his hand through his hair that needed cutting, but he hadn't taken the time. His dad would have told him it was time to clean up. The memory made his lips quirk upward. He was thirty-five years old and still missing his dad. Natalie, agent extraordinaire, had known he needed this. A wave rolled in and the sun glinting off it made it translucent. The ocean calmed him. He thought of his dad again. The loss had been devastating and he'd shoved it deep inside. Unable to face the fact that he was alone and the one man who'd been everything to him was gone.

He didn't want to talk about it, think about. Still didn't. And he knew his grief had taken his words for his books as well. Natalie had been desperate that he needed to get away and that he needed to face what had happened, for his own benefit and for his writing too. He'd been gruff with her but now he knew she'd been right. So right that somehow the words had broken loose the moment he'd walked into that upper room at Erin Sinclair's B&B. He wasn't sure he'd ever come to terms with his grief, but he knew it was at least time to face it. Soon.

He started walking slowly, his hands dug deep into his pockets. Several yards down, a dog and a woman played with a Frisbee. Closer to him, he spotted what looked like an older lady. She wore tan pants that came down just below the knees, the wide legs ruffling in the wind; a large, blue, gauzy-type shirt that covered her arms; and a bright-red hat with a wide, full brim. She was a picture. He could almost see a painting of her as she bent over and gathered seashells, or stones. She picked up one, looked at it and then, one by one, pulled her arm back and then tossed it into the ocean. He wondered what she was doing. *Skipping rocks on the ocean?* As he approached, his brain began to form a character, as often happened when certain people caught his attention. Funny what struck him at times and became inspiration. The small woman, in the big clothes and the bright-red hat, skipping rocks on the ocean inspired him.

He studied her, not sure where she would fit into his story, but still, she was there, in his head, knocking on the door, saying: "Put me in—put me in." He felt like a coach, bringing characters in from the sideline. He'd find a spot for her. He was drawing closer to her when the Frisbee sailed high in the wind and the dog suddenly barreled toward the older woman. She had her back to both the dog and Nash, and though he called out to warn her, the wind carried his voice away. He sprinted forward as the big, black dog that looked at least fifty pounds jumped into the air, intent on catching the flying disk. The dog reached the woman before Nash did and slammed into her. Woman and dog tumbled to the ground.

Nash reached them right after the disaster. Poor lady lay flat on her back. Her feet, that had been in gold-toned flip-flops, now had the flip-flops stuck straight in the air, hanging half-off her toes. Her hat was halfway across her face. The dog, just as startled by the collision as the woman, jumped up and raced away, probably fearing for its life. He'd let the owner take care of the dog. He looked down at the little lady.

"Are you okay? Let me help you."

Dazed, she looked up at him, focused, and then a smile spread across her face. "I was feeling horrible until I opened my eyes and looked up and saw this gorgeous man looking down at me."

His brows dipped and he crouched beside her. "That was a hard hit. Poor dog didn't mean to do it."

"It was a hard hit but I'm fine, a bit dizzy and sometimes there are two of your handsome face. Help me sit up and give me a minute to collect my senses and I'll be fine. Who wouldn't be fine looking at such a pretty face as yours?"

He frowned. "If you think I'm pretty, then I probably need to take you to the emergency room."

She laughed and let him help her sit up. Then she grimaced. "Ouch." She grabbed her ankle. "Oh phooey, I think my ankle is hurt."

"I am so sorry," the woman who had been throwing the Frisbee to the dog exclaimed as she reached them. "The wind caught the Frisbee, and

Samson was just going after it. I don't think he ever saw you. Are you okay?"

"I think she's hurt her ankle," Nash said, not completely wanting to get involved but not wanting to leave either.

"I have, but it's okay. You and your dog had no idea this was going to happen. It was just an accident! Please, go ahead and take your sweet dog and go on. I'll be fine."

"No, no, no. I can't possibly just walk away from this." The woman with the dog looked horrified. She held the dog back because the dog wanted to lick the older lady. Obviously, the dog was very friendly. "Do you want me to take you to the hospital? Do you need to have an x-ray?"

"No, of course not. I can walk! I'm certain I can walk."

And so he got involved. "No, you don't." He stopped her from trying to get up on her own. "Take my hand and let's see if you can put any weight on your ankle. If you can, then I'll help you get to wherever you're going. Whatever you need, I'm at your service."

"Oh, would you?"

"I'd be happy to," he said as the small lady looked at him with a mischievous or maybe even sinister smile…his imagination spun.

"How exciting. I think this is just wonderful." She lifted her hand and held it to him.

Thinking her statement was a little off, he grasped her hand and her elbow and was going to pull her up, but she grimaced.

"Maybe you need to get behind me and help. Maybe you need to put your hands under my arms or my armpits or something. I don't know, I've never had this done before. I'm really quite active. I just wasn't paying attention when the dog barreled into me and hit me just right. I feel kind of like I've been tackled playing football or something." She giggled, and he almost laughed himself.

The lady was funny. He moved behind, reached his hands under her armpits, and lifted. She popped right up, although she did not put weight on her right foot.

"So, how's that?" he asked.

She put her foot down, tried to put weight on it, then jerked it up and gasped. "It's not as good as I'd hoped. Um, maybe you can just help me get to my car. It's parked on the street there, you know, near where Main Street and Seashell cross. It's parked at the bakery, actually. Rosie's such a dear. She always lets me park my car there when I want to come down here and walk a little bit. That way it's easy access and I don't have to pay for parking. I do not understand why this small town just started having tourists pay for parking. But, it seems that everyone has got to make a dime in this day and age, and I totally understand that."

The bakery at the corner of Seashell and Main. That bakery, the one he wouldn't eat the muffins from and had spotted Erin at earlier. Of course, it would be *that* bakery. His luck had been going downhill since he got here. "Sure, I'll help you."

After they assured the lady with the dog that they would be fine, she took her dog and left.

"I'm Lila Peabody." The little lady looked up at him and smiled. "And you are Nash Bond."

He quirked a brow. "Yes, ma'am, I am." He started walking slowly with Lila, back up toward the strip. *She'd known who he was all along.*

"What is a famous author like you doing in our lovely little town?" Lila asked after they had taken a couple of steps.

"I'm here working and I'm staying here for a little while." He tried to be evasive, but he had a feeling that being evasive probably wasn't going to work. But, it was worth a try.

"You're staying somewhere?"

"I'm staying at a bed-and-breakfast in town. Not too far from here. And I'm writing."

"I expected that. I've read your books—all your books. How in the world did we get you in our community? When you first looked down at me, I thought for certain that the dog had killed me and I'd gone to heaven. You know, I look at your photo every night before I go to bed if I'm reading one of your books." She smiled at him and he suddenly felt uncomfortable. She laughed. "Just kidding. But I do love your books."

He gave a dry laugh. "You had me on that one. I'm happy you like my books."

"Just wait till I tell my friends who came to my rescue."

Nash had no doubt that she would spread the word about him being here wide and far. He bit back a groan and hoped like the dickens that people gave him space.

She looked up at him. He guessed she was about a little over five feet. Not too terribly tall. "You will love it here. I have lived here for a long time. I used to be a snowbird. I'd come down here and spend winter in this lovely weather and then me and a bunch of my friends decided to make Sunset Bay our full-time home and we love it. I'm so glad you came to visit. And you are single and there are a bunch of lovely ladies who live here."

Boy, he'd walked right into that. He hadn't meant that in terms of matchmaking schemes. He had heard that small towns sometimes had a problem with that. "It's nice that you and your friends are here. I've only been here for a couple of days, but it seems like a really nice place. Beautiful. You doing okay?"

She nodded. "This ankle, it's really bothering me. I think it's swelling more. But, none of that. We're almost there. I see the bakery from here. I'll sit down and have a cup of nice coffee, put my foot up, and I'm sure Rosie has a muffin for me. Have you had one of her muffins yet? They are absolutely to die for! May I recommend the strawberry cream cheese delight? They are just absolutely out of this world."

Those muffins again. "I haven't tried the muffins, but I'll probably have to."

"Have to? You'll be grateful you did. When we get there, I'll treat you to as many as you want and a cup of coffee. Or whatever else you want to drink. But you look like you're a coffee drinker. And Rosie has delicious coffee, although if you're staying at Erin's place... You are staying at Erin's place, aren't you? It's the best in town and she is just a dear. And beautiful. And single."

Had he told her he was at Erin's place? He didn't remember that. "Um, I'm there. But, you know, I'm in my little attic area room. I'm holed up. I'll be up there writing."

As if she hadn't heard him, she rattled on. "Erin's a lovely person. And beautiful, don't you think?"

"Yes, ma'am, she is." He could feel a trap coming.

"We have a summer festival this weekend and some fundraisers coming up, too, while you are here. I'm hoping you'll join us at them. How long will you be here?"

"At least a couple of months. I'm trying to finish a book, and sometimes it takes awhile to finish a book." He didn't mention that he probably wouldn't finish the book in two months, but at least if he maybe got himself back on track with his writing, it wouldn't be much longer than that.

"Lovely. Well, you know, all work and no play will make a dull boy. And you know, getting out and getting involved will get your creative juices flowing, I'm sure. We have all kinds of things coming up, like summer festivals, and well, you've already missed the firefighter fundraiser that we had to raise money for our firefighters. Did you know that Erin's brother,

Brad, is the fire chief? He's a really nice guy. He's marrying a good friend of ours. And Erin's other brother is the town doctor, and he married Rosie, she owns the bakery where we're going to have a muffin and one of those lovely cups of coffee. I'm sure that you will enjoy meeting them. They're guys I think you'll get along with quite well, and they like to do all kinds of things. I think we're having a crab festival, you know, where everyone comes down to the water and we all throw our crab traps out. Have you ever crabbed?"

"I have crabbed only once in my life. That's where I throw that little crab trap out in the water with a chicken leg on it and the crabs all try to eat. I pull 'em up and get one."

"Exactly! You'll have to come on out and give it a try."

They had reached the bakery. He glanced around and saw the three ladies sitting on the other side of the door, just around the curved sidewalk. Just for a moment, he thought he was safe. Just for a moment, he was out of their view.

And then, Erin spotted him and Lila.

The moment Erin saw Lila and Nash, she thought she was seeing things. But then she realized he was helping Lila walk. She nearly dropped her cup of coffee. She jumped to her feet. Rosie and Lulu turned to see what she saw and sprang to their feet too.

"Lila?" They all exclaimed and hurried toward her.

Erin was concerned for her friend, but her gaze locked with that of Nash Bond. He looked wary but he also looked great. He had changed out of his dress clothing and into shorts and he wore a bold blue T-shirt that complemented the man's eyes. *Why was she noticing the man's eyes?*

She dragged her eyes away from him and looked at Lila as she approached her. "What happened? Are you okay?"

"I'm fine. I just fell. A cute little dog tripped me and I fell. I fell on sand, but somehow I still hurt my ankle, and this wonderful, wonderful man helped me."

"She did everything that she said she did. Can we sit her down here?" he asked, trying not to focus on all the women fluttering around.

"Yes, please," Rosie said. "Sit her right here and, here, put her foot up. We'll look at it."

"A dog tripped you?" Lulu asked. Seeing as Lulu owned a dog walking service and had opened the new pet B&B recently, she was always concerned about dogs. Even misbehaving dogs.

"Oh, don't worry, Lulu. It wasn't one of your dogs. It was a tourist's dog. A large but adorable black ball of fluff and they were playing Frisbee and I was over there looking at seashells when the dog got carried away running and knocked my legs out from underneath me. It scared the poor dog as much as it scared me. But, you know, good things come from bad things. Just look at this handsome young man who came to my rescue—Nash Bond."

Nash had this look on his face of wanting to crawl under a rock somewhere. Erin felt for him, actually. If the man thought that he was going to come to this small little town and actually disappear and not be noticed… First of all, he couldn't go anywhere and not be noticed simply because of the man he was. Second, with as many books as the man sold, his face was plastered all over everything. And having been probably one of the only authors in the world to be stuck on the front of *People Magazine* as most eligible bachelor, he was recognizable.

"Yes, Lila," she said. "We know who he is. He's staying at the B&B. And I think he's here for some peace and quiet, so I mean, you might ask him. He might not want you walking around and telling everyone who he is." There. She at least had tried. He couldn't be grouchy at her and he wouldn't be able to say that she was the one who had spread word he was here, because she hadn't. All she had told was Lulu and Rosie and her family that he was coming.

"Very nice to meet you." Lulu smiled at Nash as if she hadn't heard anything just a few moments ago from Erin about the man.

Erin bit her lip, holding back the smile that threatened to burst forward. Lulu, bless her heart, was putting on a good show when she knew what a grouch he had been. Erin hadn't held back with these two. Lulu and Rosie both knew what she thought about the man. Well, they knew what she had told them, but they both had other ideas. She was going to have to speak to them about that.

"I've heard of you." Rosie smiled. "And I've read your books, too. However, I have to say, I find myself reading more romances these days. I like happy endings, and in the last book that I read, you killed off one of the main characters unnecessarily. I just can't handle that."

The man blinked and stared at Rosie, as if the man thought that killing off a main character was not a big deal. Erin had to admit, she, too, liked books where you could read them and not worry about the person that you had invested all your time in and grown to care for suddenly meeting a bad ending. Life had too much of that on its own. She didn't want to read about it and she was pretty sure that was why Rosie felt that way too.

She did not want to read a book that scared her or that she bawled her eyes out for the wrong reason.

"Oh, girls." Lila sighed. "I love that adventure and drama that happens in his books. You never know if it's going to be an adventure, a mystery, a thriller. He's one of those multi-talented authors who can just pull you in and make you believe. And oh, his words! He's just an excellent, excellent writer. You must give him another chance if you haven't read one of his latest books."

Erin bit her lip again. "Rosie, why don't we go inside? Maybe you should call Adam or Brad."

"Yes, I'll do that. Inside, everyone, and Lulu—you help Mr. Bond get Lila comfortable. Erin—you come help me get coffee and muffins for everyone while I call Adam."

With that, they all went inside.

Rosie suddenly turned with a pretty smile plastered to her face. "Please, Mr. Bond, take a seat. We will be right back. How do you take your coffee? Or do you take iced coffee? Or do you like caramel mochas? Erin loves caramel mochas. They are quite good."

Why in the world was she telling him what her favorite coffee was? She would have elbowed her if Nash hadn't been staring at them.

His brows dipped. "Thank you, Rosie. I'll just take a black coffee. And will you throw in one of those…" He hesitated and looked at Lila. "What was the one you suggested, Lila?"

Lila beamed. "He wants a strawberry cream cheese delight, and I'll have one, too! And I'm paying for his. I told him I'd treat him for being such a dear and getting me up here."

Erin felt steam shooting from her ears and nostrils. The man ate Rosie's muffins, just not when *she* brought him Rosie's muffins.

"Perfect. Coming right up," Rosie exclaimed and then grabbed Erin by the arm and dragged her with her behind the counter and back to the back room, out of sight.

The man was pushing her buttons, he was. But she

couldn't afford to explode. Besides, he had rescued her friend.

Gigi was getting supplies from the back room when they entered. "Hey, what's up? Are you all finished chatting? Because I'm doing okay by myself right now."

"No, Gigi, we've got an emergency. Lila has hurt herself and so I'm going to call Adam and then grab some coffee and muffins. Could you give us a few minutes and fill a cup with black coffee for the good-looking man with Lila? And make one the way that Lila likes hers, too."

"Sure thing." Gigi headed out and left them alone.

Rosie had her phone. "Stay right there. Do not move." She pressed a button on her phone and then spoke to Adam's receptionist at the clinic, asking whether he was available to talk. "He's setting a broken arm," she said. "Okay, could you tell him when he's finished and has the time, Lila Peabody has hurt her ankle and is here at the coffee shop, if he could come by when he can. I'll call Brad, so he might be able to get here first. Thanks."

"I think Lulu was calling him," Erin said.

"Great. Maybe he can come immediately. And you, girl—that man's pictures do not do him justice. And he is staying at your B&B. Girlfriend, there has *got* to be some chemistry between you two. I felt it the moment your eyes met his."

"Rosie, don't get carried away. I told you, he is hard to handle."

She smiled. "And that might be interesting. Sparks are fun."

Erin rubbed her temple. "Rosie, let's just get the muffins. And please drop this because your ideas are not going to happen." She walked back into the front of the bakery and headed toward the tray that Gigi had set up for them. "Thank you. I'll take this."

As she carried the tray toward the table, she tried to get herself to calm down. But all she could think about was that if Rosie was thinking this and Lila had a twinkle in her eyes, then what would her friends Doreen, Mami, and Birdie think? She feared she was now going to have to fend off their assumptions. *Please, no.*

Erin's stomach kind of soured, thinking about them. She hoped they didn't start getting any ideas about her and the hunk of man—the barbarian—sitting there with Lila. What would she do if the four of them started to jump on the "let's get Erin hitched" train or the "let's get Erin a date" train? Surely, they wouldn't get carried away with something like that. Just because they had been interested in Brad and Lulu getting together didn't mean that they were starting to get this itch. At least, she prayed they didn't.

He was here for two months and then he was leaving. Butterflies were not enough to get over his bad attitude. She wasn't sure that she was going to be able to handle being under the same roof with him for that long. It was going to take a whole lot of pep talks to keep her focused on keeping him happy so she'd get that good review. She needed the visibility and he'd just been placed in her path out of the blue, right when she needed the exposure his being here could give her.

Despite the festival happening that weekend, she only had a few rooms booked—two, other than his—when she had three more that could have been utilized, though they weren't completely finished as she wanted them to be. The last two had a long way to go. She had to keep her thoughts focused and not let herself get riled up by something as small as him eating muffins offered by someone else and not by her.

It was so childish. And those butterflies—well, she was ignoring them already.

CHAPTER SIX

From his balcony, Nash could see the people getting ready for the crabbing festival, and he was amazed at how the sleepy little town of yesterday had morphed into the tourist trap that it was now. Roads were blocked, people were everywhere, and a lot of them had little crabbing nets with them that looked like giant fly swatters made out of chicken wire. He had heard laughter and he had smelled that caramel corn again. He might not be a huge sweet eater, but he liked caramel corn. He had actually been sitting on the balcony, writing and watching the people gathering around and setting up tents to sell their wares. And though the balcony of his room was on the side of the house and he couldn't see the front door exit, he actually glimpsed Erin leave the house a few minutes ago, walk across the street, and down toward the festivities.

She wore white shorts and a yellow-and-white striped top and looked neat and summery with her long blonde hair and the bright-blue beach bag she had slung over her shoulder. He wondered what she had in that bag. He wondered whether she was going crabbing.

They hadn't spoken since the day at the bakery. Now, he had the unshakable thought of seeking her out at the festival and trying to make peace with her.

After leaving Lila in the capable hands of all her friends, he had left the bakery and gone back to the inn. He'd had Erin on his mind but he'd fought the thoughts off and thrown himself back into his work, determined not to be distracted. Not that it would matter to her that he'd been thinking about her. Thinking about the anger he'd seen in her eyes when he'd enjoyed those muffins after not having eaten the ones she'd offered him on his first day at the inn. He'd been a brute, determined to get his way and he had, all right. Because obviously, she had gotten the hint. She hadn't bothered him at all the last few days. The water and the carafe of coffee would show up outside his door but he never caught her leaving it. And whenever he did go down for coffee or to forage in the refrigerator for something to eat, she was never around. She was conspicuously absent.

He had enjoyed meeting her brother Brad, the fire chief, when he'd come to the bakery to look at Lila's ankle. Brad had invited him to join them for crabbing and to meet his brothers. He wondered what Erin would think if he showed up. She hadn't said much that day when he and Brad were talking. And now, the temptation to join the festivities pulled hard at him. He should, after all, get the feel of the place considering he might want the experience for a book sometime. But as he stood and closed his computer, he knew this had nothing to do with research.

He changed into fresh clothes—a shirt, shorts, and

a pair of boat shoes—then headed out the front door with his hands in his pockets. He strolled down the street the direction Erin had gone and toward the scent of caramel corn. Today he would have some and hopefully, he'd run into Erin. What he would do, he wasn't sure, but it bothered him more and more what she thought of him. That he was a spoiled, demanding grouch, probably, and it was well deserved. But, he wasn't always and it was time he fixed this mess he'd made.

He would walk down to the beach and watch people throw traps into the water and see whether they could catch some blue crabs. He hadn't gone far when he saw the caramel corn truck. It was a beautiful sight and his mouth watered. But what was even more beautiful was the blonde with the yellow-and-white striped shirt and white shorts, holding the blue bag as she stood at the window of the caramel corn truck, about to order.

If he had wanted to run into her, this was his chance. Taking a deep breath, he headed that way. She didn't see him as he walked up. "If that's half as good as it smells, it'll be fantastic."

She spun to look at him, startled as she stared at him. He smiled when she didn't speak. "You like caramel corn?"

She nodded, her eyes sparkling. "I do. Do *you*?"

He gave a half smile. "I'm hurt. Not even a 'Hello, how are you?' for your favorite houseguest?"

She looked embarrassed. "Sorry, I…of course I'm glad to see you. And it's really good caramel corn."

She remained uptight.

"Look, Erin. I wouldn't have smiled either. I've put you in a bad situation. I started us out on the wrong footing and I'm sorry. How about I buy you that caramel corn and we start over?"

She held his gaze, and he could see her thoughts whirling behind those pretty blue eyes.

He tried again. "I promise, I'm not as bad as I've led you to believe. But I wouldn't blame you if you told me to get lost."

She sighed. "I wouldn't do that. I am your hostess. And it is my job to let the customer always be right. So, if you say that you aren't as hard to please as you've obviously pretended to be, then, as your hostess, it is my duty to believe you. Therefore, I will let you buy my caramel corn, and we will call it a truce."

Her sardonic answer made him laugh. She had a sense of humor. "Great. Then, let's do this." He stepped up to the window. "I'll have two extra-large bags. Do you want anything to drink?"

"No, I won't have enough hands to eat and drink."

"True. That's it then," he told the guy, paid him and then took the bags. "Here you go."

She took her bag and he smiled. "Thank you. So far you're doing well starting over."

He bit into a piece of sticky caramel corn and smiled at her as it melted in his mouth. "This right here will make anything seem better. Even me."

"I think you might be right about that."

Using her fingers, Erin dug a few pieces of caramel corn from her paper bag and placed them in her mouth and considered the man walking beside her. She had left him alone the last few days purposefully, just like he'd instructed her to. She'd worked in the garage on the furniture she was refinishing and tried to let him have the house to himself. A few times, she'd heard him coming down the stairs and had actually hidden in the laundry room, and other times she'd made it out the back door and into her garden. It had felt completely weird to hide in her own home but if he wanted his space, she wanted him to have it. The last thing she wanted him to do was come into the kitchen and find her in there. She hadn't been ready to see him anyway.

She had really hoped he was getting his writing done. She was curious about what was going on in that room upstairs. Was he actually able to create? She hoped so.

She had seen a different side of him the day he'd rescued Lila. He had actually been very nice to Lila and very congenial to everyone else who had been there.

"So, how was your day today?" He then took a bite of his caramel corn.

"It was good. I got a lot accomplished."

"What did you get accomplished? You had a couple of guests come in this morning, I saw. Very quiet people."

She laughed. "And you appreciate very quiet people. Yes, the older couples who checked in are here for a quiet weekend of crabbing. So you don't have anything to worry about."

"I didn't say I was worried. Happy that they were quiet, yes, but not worried. I'm very certain that if you had some unruly guests that you could take care of it."

"Well, isn't that a nice thing to say. So how was your day?"

"It was decent. I got a few thousand words written and I went down to a little taco stand with a few chairs and tables sitting around, and I had a very productive lunch alone. I listened to the seagulls, smelled the salt air, and had me a very nice drink and tacos while I worked on plot scenarios. And then I came back to the room and put them on paper."

"You typed them really hard on the computer?"

He stopped walking and stared at her. "Yes, as a matter of fact I did. So you're telling me that you stand by the door and listen to see if I'm typing?"

She smiled. "Of course not. I was carrying linens up to the second floor and I could hear a tapping noise. You type really hard."

"I do. It's not something I can stop and the faster I'm typing, trying to get the words out, the harder I type."

"I was in my garden this morning and heard you on the balcony."

"You were in your garden? I didn't see you this time."

She stopped walking. "You've seen me?"

"Yes, I saw you humming while you watered your plants that second day I was here."

"Oh. I didn't see you."

"I didn't want to interrupt you."

"And I didn't want to interrupt you this morning."

He held her gaze. "I'm sorry you didn't. But I take full responsibility for that. Don't let me keep you from your garden."

Who was this man and what had he done with Nash Bond?

They walked for a few minutes, both observing everything that was going on around them at the festival. People were coming and going and looking at various booths, grabbing funnel cakes and lemonade and hot dogs and frozen ice cream. Kids ran around and beach music played. It was a great atmosphere. Erin always enjoyed the festivals that her little town put on. They had been thinking about hiring an events planner because the town had grown and the events were starting to become more and more important to draw tourists to town. The mayor and the city manager were thinking that it might pay for them to hire someone to do the social media and the event planning versus hiring it out on an as-needed basis. She was beginning to think it was a good idea.

And though she liked her small town, Sunset Bay could use the revenue. Her livelihood was dependent on it, and so many of the shops could use the business of the tourists coming to town. A B&B needed tourists. "What brought you to Sunset Bay? There's so many beautiful locations in Florida. The coastline is endless. Just up the street—well, not up the street, but not too terribly far from here is St. Pete's Beach and also Windswept Bay, and farther down Barefoot Bay and Naples, and across the way is Melbourne. And, of course, the Keys are gorgeous. Too many places to mention and you came here. There's just a lot of beautiful places and you end up here in my B&B in Sunset Bay?"

He was munching down on the caramel corn. The man obviously loved caramel corn because he was digging into it faster than she was. He looked a tad sheepish. "Sorry, I have a weakness for this stuff. I'm being a little bit of a hog."

She laughed, actually enjoying seeing this side of him. She made a note to herself: she would gather several boxes of that before this festival was over and give him a little surprise. She could be a very good hostess.

"I actually didn't request Sunset Bay. I requested a small coastal town, fairly quaint, with atmosphere. Natalie found Sunset Bay and your honeymoon suite."

She slowed her pace, thinking. "Well, I'm wondering where she saw it. I mean, I've done some social media, but I'd really… Maybe I'll call her, or would you mind asking her where she might have seen it at? Because if I can zero in on what type of advertising I'm doing that is actually working, then maybe I can up the dollars in that area. It would be very helpful. I guess you've noticed that my B&B is fairly new. It hasn't been open much more than a few months. Nearly three, actually. And it's not completely renovated, so it's been a little bit of a challenge getting ready. I opened because I thought, you know, that it would be good for me to hone my skills and if I had some great reviews prior to opening full force, then it would be great to have those reviews there and helpful."

If he only knew how helpful.

She hadn't had someone in the B&B every weekend, and she wasn't completely booked right now. She still had a couple of weekends, actually. The next two coming up were still vacant, but there wasn't a festival going on other than this one and nothing extra to draw people in other than getting away and coming to Sunset Beach.

There apparently weren't any weddings going on. There were a couple of wedding venues, but she hadn't yet gotten the overflow from those. She was hoping that when the wedding season came full force, she would but it would be nice to be one of their top places to be recommended.

"I'll ask Natalie. I'm sure she'll tell us and if not, then I'll goad it out of her. But I'm pretty positive she'll tell us where she discovered your place."

"Thank you. It very well could be that she looked at several places and she saw a picture of the honeymoon suite, saw a description, and saw a picture of the fairly private garden below it. I guess you've figured out that's my private garden. That's the garden off my quarters. So, it allows for a very private and quiet little getaway on that balcony. Maybe she saw that and..." she thought about it for a second, "and she might have seen that I don't have it fully booked. There are several weekends that are vacant. As a matter of fact, the two couples I have there now who you haven't met since you have been holed up in your room…" She couldn't help herself. She shot him a slightly satirical smile. She wanted to goad him. "Anyway, they're my only clients besides you for the next three weeks unless something suddenly happens and spur-of-the-moment people call. So, just so you know, I'm actually very grateful that you're here and it's another reason that I'm trying so desperately to be a good hostess to you. And do it your way. I assume I tried a little too hard the day you checked in and hovered too much."

He placed a hand on her arm and her skin instantly warmed from his touch. Her eyes locked with his as he stopped her in the middle of the crowd. His expression was intense.

"You didn't do anything wrong. It was me. I'm frustrated with myself, and I was overbearing and it was uncalled for. All you did was try to be a good hostess. I refused those muffins just because I was determined to prove a point. I have to tell you, after meeting Lila and coming up to the bakery and eating that strawberry cream cheese delight, you were right—it was out of this world. I plan to try all of the bakery's flavors before I leave. So please, stop blaming yourself."

"Wow, you're actually a nice guy. I am impressed. You are not like all the men I've known. You actually came clean on the truth and you apologized. I never expected that."

His forehead wrinkled, as if he were perplexed by her.

Maybe she shouldn't have said that part aloud. "But I am your hostess, and again, I have to go with what I normally go with, and that is that the client is always right. In this instance, I'll just agree with you and say that you are absolutely right on all counts. You were overbearing. And you did get your point across."

A huge smile burst to his lips and then he laughed.

And it was a really nice sound.

His hand, still on her arm, tightened before he pulled it away. "I think on that particular point, you were very glad to tell me that the client is always right. I'm glad I gave you something you can agree with me on."

The breeze ruffled her hair and his too. She watched the dark bangs that he'd swept from his forehead several times now lifted playfully in the breeze, teasing her fingers to smooth it down. She didn't and pushed the thought away with force. But her mood lifted and her spirits, too. She'd come to the festival to try to get out of the funk she'd been in and now admitted that all day, while she had forced herself to stay away from him, she had wanted very much to see him. To check on him, she amended, determined to believe that any interest she had in the complex man was simply because he was her guest.

Not comfortable just standing there staring at him, she started walking once more toward the water in the distance and went to safer conversation. "Do you want to do some crabbing?"

She could see her family in the distance, gathered on the beach, enjoying the fun. Almost all of them were there, and she figured if she took him down there and introduced him to them, he might be overwhelmed, but oh well. He was here and maybe wanted to get a taste of the flavor of Sunset Bay. There was no better flavor than her family, being loud and fun. "My family is over there but I warn you—there is no telling what they'll say or do. But they love crabbing. It's a family passion."

"Sure. I'm not the greatest at crabbing, but I've observed it a few times. I'm not actually the greatest fisherman but I enjoy it. I'm more of a Hemmingway and Zane Grey fisherman, though. Nowhere as good or as passionate as those legendary authors but, like them I prefer deep sea fishing instead of wade fishing from the shore."

"Of course you are. I would think standing on the beach or the side of a lake and waiting on a bite is a little too tame for you. I put you and my brother Tate in the same category, with needing a shot of adrenaline from some risky hobby in order to make you enjoy it."

That visibly startled him momentarily. Maybe because she'd read him correctly. The man could sit for hours writing but there was a restless nature to him that she recognized, even if she hadn't heard about his escapades in the articles she'd read. Her brother Tate had that same restlessness and it always scared her. She'd had to learn to keep her thoughts to herself where Tate's need for adventure was concerned. She worried about him but had learned to manage it with the words he always said to her: that he was well trained, didn't take unnecessary risks, and for her to not worry. Looking at Nash, she suddenly was reminded of their differences. They were opposites in every way.

He finally shrugged and gave a smile. "That'd be me."

Her nerves rattled at the very idea of doing things this man thought were fun. She needed her feet to be firmly connected to the earth, unless she was riding in a large commercial plane with a great safety record. Despite that, the boyish gleam that came into Nash's eyes when thinking about his love of adventurous activities caused the unwanted butterflies to flutter in her chest again. She fought to ignore them and pasted on a smile.

"Then come along. Believe me, you have much more in common with my brothers than you do with me. I'll introduce you."

Nash fell into step with Erin. She intrigued him more and more. He'd seen the moment of nervousness, or fear that had shadowed her eyes when talking about her brother's love of risky hobbies. He assumed she would call anything that was more adventurous than reading a book risky. And that fake smile she'd pasted on was nothing like her genuine smile. He really liked that smile. It was as though it cut through some of the murk that shrouded him these days. He realized he would like to see it more often versus the frown that he had brought to her face every time he'd been around her since their first meeting.

"Well, when in Sunset Bay, do as they do and you will have fun. That's my family straight ahead. If you don't mind meeting the horde, then come along. I have several brothers and a sister. Cassie's actually in town, so you'll get to meet her. She's not usually here. And

Tate is here too. His visits are few and far in between. They both usually travel extensively with their careers, so this is kind of a grand moment for us when we have everybody here at one time."

"So that's not a common thing?"

"Not exactly. You've met Brad and then, if you remember, my brother Adam is the new doctor. He was a big-time trauma doctor in New York, Chicago, and I think LA and we didn't see much of him for several years. Finally, he had a sort of crisis and came home a couple months ago, and we were so excited about that. And then he took the job with the local doctor and fell for Rosie, and that put my mother on cloud nine. She had recently gotten the itch for grandchildren and we were all feeling the pressure of her wanting us to marry and give her what she wants. Adam and Rosie and now Brad and Lulu have taken some of the heat off the rest of us. Anyway, my other brother is Jonah—if you get the urge to take a boat out, he owns Jonah's Boat Rentals. You know, the one with the logo of the whale spitting the little dude out?"

He laughed. "I've seen that. Cute logo. Did your

brother change his name to Jonah just for that, or did it just work out?"

"It just worked out. From day one, he was interested in boats. He tore down every small piece of equipment my dad owned. Our boat we owned growing up was always in pieces as he worked on it and discovered out how to put boats together, how to take them apart again and again, and he started fixing boats early. I mean, I don't even know if he was out of eighth grade when he started repairing boats for friends. Now, he has a successful business, and it's great because he's very local. Anyway, too much information I'm sure, but I love them all dearly and I think you'll really get along with them. They'll loan you a crabbing trap. They have plenty. Oh, and Lulu—did I forget to mention Lulu? You met her at the bakery. She's marrying Brad. She might be down there. I'm trying to look for the red hair, but she might have too many dogs at her doggie B&B. She might be stuck tonight. Which, she doesn't mind being stuck. She loves all her dogs."

"I remember her. She was good with Lila and

when Brad arrived, it was obvious that she and he were in love."

She looked startled. "You noticed that?"

He laughed. "I am an author. Observing people is just part of my nature."

"Of course." She cocked her head and turned serious. "You might read people easily but I have to tell you that you are really hard to read."

He nodded lightly. "Just the way I want it."

CHAPTER SEVEN

"**H**ey Nash, so you decided to join us," Brad called out as they approached. He wore cargo shorts and a faded red T-shirt that said, *Who you gonna call?* He was holding a crab trap and grinning.

"Yeah, I did. Sitting up there on my balcony and hearing and seeing everything going on down here on the street kept drawing my attention away from my book. And then I could smell the caramel corn the instant they cranked up the caramel corn machine and that was the last straw. I closed the computer and headed down here. I found your sister at the caramel corn trailer, so here I am."

Brad nodded at the caramel corn. "That'll do it. Glad you're here. Of course, this is a motley crew, my family. You've met Erin, your faithful B&B hostess, and I'll let each of my brothers introduce themselves and the rest of my family."

One of the men stepped forward. He had sandy-brown hair and lean features. "Welcome. I'm Adam. I want to thank you for helping Lila the other afternoon. Rosie, my wife, called me from the bakery but Brad got there before I could. By the time I arrived, you had already left. I'm thankful you were there to help her."

"Nice to meet you. I'm glad I was there too. And I'm glad she's better. I bet it's an ordeal to keep her off it, though. She's a go-getter."

"You have no idea. You put her and her three lady friends together and they keep this town on its toes."

Another man jogged over from the edge of the water. He had similar sandy brown hair as Adam. He wore board shorts and no shirt that showed off a six-pack and muscled upper chest that clearly took a lot of work. Brad and Adam were in shape. Nash stayed in shape too, but he didn't spend the kind of time on it that a physique like this would take.

"I'm Tate. I read your books. You're about the only author I read, so I couldn't believe it when I heard you were here in town and staying at Erin's. I bet you won't find any intrigue or adventure books on the B&B bookshelves. *Some* people stress out from anything that has to do with anything with an uncertain ending."

Nash grinned and caught Erin's gaze and winked. "Yeah, I've figured that out. But I guess to each his own."

"I told you, I just don't like uncertain endings. You kill too many of your characters off. I read a couple—well, actually, I'm fibbing. I read one. But I read the reviews and, um, decided to give up on them."

He laughed. "At least you're honest."

"Erin is always honest. I'm Jonah." The last brother came up. He had black hair and was as tall as the others, broader, and very laid-back, Nash decided. Jonah Sinclair looked like a man who enjoyed life. "I actually don't read much. I prefer to do something with my hands to relax. Too busy tearing things apart and putting them back together. But, I'll take your word for it."

"No problem. To each his own. I wouldn't know the first thing about tearing something apart. Erin told me you have boats. I might come out and rent one." He hitched a brow at Erin. "Would you go for a ride with me?"

Erin went still. "I…" She paused, her forehead crinkled.

"Sure, she will." A woman came up, carrying a crab trap full of crabs. Nash knew this was Cassie because she looked enough like Erin that it had to be her sister.

"Cassie, I don't—"

"Have anything to do tomorrow? You told me that when we talked about having lunch. So go. I have other plans and can't have lunch with you." Cassie winked at Nash, and he chuckled at how transparent she was.

"Looks like your schedule is free and your guest

needs a guide on the boat." He smiled, feeling a little wicked as he challenged her with his look.

"Fine. I'll go with you."

"Perfect." He grinned and Cassie did too.

"She has been working so hard on her B&B that I don't think she's taken much time off in months. This will be good for her. You are totally not her type. I read your books and know what kind of a lifestyle you have. I have been known to jump out of an airplane myself. Erin likes everything in its place and she's pretty cautious."

"Cassie!" Erin gasped.

Cassie laughed and kept on talking. "But I hear opposites attract. Have you ever thought about putting a little romance in your books? Kind of crossing the line a little bit, shaking things up?"

Erin's sister was bold and nothing like her. He liked her. But he had no idea what she was getting at. "My books have some romance in them, but more of the *Bourne* series kind of romance where if the romance is working out by the end, it's usually not working out by book two or movie two."

"Exactly. I've seen that." Cassie smiled. "But, I mean, is that how you are in your real life? Leaving a wake of broken hearts behind you? Romance ends with a happily-ever-after and it stays that way."

Brad grinned. "Cassie has no problem saying what she's thinking. You might need to run."

"Ignore them," Erin said. "I told you they were something,"

He gave her a half smile. "I'm pretty set in my ways too." He was not going to stand here in this crowd and talk about his love life. Cassie and Erin might be sisters, but they were different. Then again, he just got the feeling that they were all fishing. And he wasn't talking crabbing. They were curious. He wondered whether Erin picked up on that.

The older couple who had been busy farther down the beach pulling in crab traps now hurried up. "Nash Bond. It is so exciting to have you here. I'm Marietta and this is my husband Leo. We're the parents of this crazy crew."

"It's nice to meet you both."

He shook Leo's hand and they all talked about his

books and him being here at Sunset Bay.

Leo busied himself pulling crabs off the crab trap. "You better watch out for my Marietta. She'll soon be talking you into making this the setting of one of your books."

"True," Tate said. "Or having a romance at least." Then out of the corner of his mouth, he muttered, "Our mother has become obsessed. If you know what I mean."

Erin looked mortified and Nash was getting the idea.

"All right, everybody." Erin grabbed his arm. "A hundred questions is over. It's time to let Nash do some crabbing. And you know every one of you are really good at it, so somebody hand him a crabbing trap and a chicken leg."

Brad handed him a crab trap. "Here you go. After we've caught the crabs, we're all going to get together and cook them. You're welcome to join us, or you can bring them back to your B&B and hopefully talk your hostess into cooking them for you."

Erin looked a little exasperated with her family.

"Your hostess can do whatever you'd like. If you'd like to eat with my family, that would be great, or if you'd like me to cook them for you, I can do that. I'm actually a very good cook, despite the fact that you have yet to find that out."

He smiled. "I deserved that. And I might have to take you up on that."

She put a hand to her heart. "Oh, be still my heart. I can hardly wait."

He laughed again and took the spoiled chicken leg that Adam handed him. He opened the crab trap, which was a hinged contraption with a flat basket that just opened. You slipped the chicken leg inside so that the wire came back together, and then you threw it using the rope it was tied to as far as you could into the water or wherever you thought the crabs were and let the crabs come to it. He was ready for this, and he figured he was probably going to be terrible at it.

"Erin, you know good and well you're really good at this, so take him over there and show him how it's done." Cassie gave her sister a little shove. "It's true— she can out-crab anybody, even Jonah, and Jonah is one of the best crabbers out here."

"Hey," Brad said, "I do good."

"In your dreams." Cassie laughed. "Erin, this is in your wheelhouse, and he's your guest, so do this."

Erin inhaled and looked resigned to the fact that she was about to be an instructor to the grouchy boarder. He, on the other hand, was actually happy about the turn of events.

"You got one!" Erin exclaimed twenty minutes later when he pulled the rope and towed in the crab trap covered with large blue crab.

"Only because I think your family is right—you're a great teacher. Now for the tricky part—getting them off there without getting our fingers pinched."

She laughed. "Well, you're right, you do have to be careful. They really know how to hurt you. Unlike a snow crab that can't do as much damage, these can. You definitely want to keep little kids' fingers away from them. So, let's just be careful."

"Oh, I will be. I'm planning to use these fingers for typing later. I need them."

Working together, they plucked the crabs off of the trap and then dropped them into a five-gallon bucket with water. They stood close as they worked and when Erin turned her head to smile at him, he wanted to dip his lips to hers. Until that moment, he'd never, ever thought crabbing could be a romantic endeavor. Looking into her eyes, he knew he'd been wrong.

She suddenly stood back, put her hands on her hips, and nodded at the trap. "It's time to heft that thing back out there and into the water if you want more crabs."

He grinned at her, knowing he'd made her nervous. He wondered whether she'd thought about kissing him too.

He checked the trap to make sure it was closed. Then, holding the end of the long rope, he slung the trap out and watched it sail across the water until it made a splash. He had set a stake into the sand and he tied a rope around it. Standing there with all the other people dotting the beach waiting, with several feet between them so their lines wouldn't get tangled, it felt as if he and Erin were basically alone.

"I guess everybody was right—you do know what you're doing."

"I've always been lucky."

"Whatever it is, I like it. So what made you want to open up a B&B?"

She smiled and tucked a flying strand of hair behind her ear. "I was in the corporate world and bored out of my mind. I was living here and driving into Tampa every day and it was, uh, you know, a little over an hour and a half drive; depending on traffic, sometimes two hours. I wanted to be here, and I was tired of sitting at a desk and staring out a window and wishing for more freedom. So, I asked myself, what could I do? And a B&B was the logical thing because I enjoy people. And this house was just sitting there, dying. And every time I passed by it, I felt a little overwhelmed by the way it looked. I could hardly stand it. And so I came home one Friday, called the Realtor and met him there to look at it. From my childhood, I can remember when it was in fairly decent shape. The owners, an older couple, tried to take care of it, but a house that size isn't easily taken care of on a fixed budget and it had started to deteriorate. I always thought that it was beautiful. I had some money saved and decided to go for it."

"Well, well, well, you aren't as cautious and adventure phobic as everyone says you are."

She bit back a smile. "My family thought I was crazy at first, especially because, as you have been told, I am a creature of habit and I don't like not knowing what's going to happen. I am not excited about surprises, especially bad surprises, and you know, when you go into debt all by yourself, it's a bit scary. I really don't know what came over me. Some days I'm really terrified it's all going to fail."

"Really? Why would you think that?"

"I need business and cash flow. I don't know if it's going to be a good or a bad outcome. I'm hoping with the final transformation and good reviews—and if I could be a very good hostess—that I'll get repeat customers. And a good outcome. That's what I'm planning on, anyway…" A wishful look filled her eyes and it had him feeling the need she was expressing. "I want it to be a success, so I need for my B&B to do well. I need to make those payments. I have savings, but it's not endless. And, well, I can be too pushy sometimes, I've realized. I need everyone who comes to leave a good review and want to come back. I hope I haven't smothered others with my determination to be the best hostess."

Her longing had shifted to a worry and he felt a hard fist of guilt. "You're a good hostess, Erin. You're going to be okay. You proved it in dealing with me and my bad attitude. I hope I didn't cause you to worry more about not being a good hostess. I was just worried about my ability to produce work and was having a bad day." He paused, the truth clogging his throat. He hadn't discussed his past with anyone. Natalie knew some of it because she'd guessed his grief was the reason he'd stalled but he had never told her.

"I understa—"

"No, you don't. In this past year, I've had more bad days than good..." He tried to be honest but he wasn't the kind of man who spilled his guts to anyone. He'd once been a vulnerable kid on the streets who'd been cast away by the ones who were supposed to love him. He'd been desperate and done what he needed to survive. He closed the past off, knowing he couldn't open those wounds. "It seems like I've gotten myself into a rut. But that is no reason for me to have been so rough on you. I'm going to do better."

She stared hard at him, as if she'd known that hadn't been what he'd planned to say. "You are very unpredictable."

He grinned at her, determined to shake the claws of the past off this conversation. "I have to keep you on your toes."

She laughed, relaxing. "Oh, don't worry—you do that with flying colors."

"You keep me off-balance too, you know, and I'm not used to that." That was true. He'd never had a woman make him feel this odd sense of frustration and protection at the same time. He'd never been drawn to a woman like this either. Her blue gaze pulled at him.

"What do you mean?"

He wanted to pull her into his arms and kiss her. To feel her there against him, her heart beating against his, solid and luring his own heart to feel more than he'd known it could. Instead, he tugged gently at a strand of her long, silky hair. "Every time you smile at me that way, I feel the need to smile back. And that isn't something I'm used to."

"Oh…well, that's nice. You need to smile more. You have a…a very nice smile."

"Really?" He teased her, hitting a brow and grinning because he couldn't help it. She blushed and her eyes had moved to his lips. He wondered whether she was thinking about kissing his lips like he was thinking about kissing hers.

"Um, yes." She then turned to the water. "You

better pull that trap in."

She was right to change the subject. He knew it and had no idea why he had been pushing her when the last thing he needed was to complicate his stay here with getting personal with his beautiful innkeeper.

But as he studied her profile, he knew that he was going to have a very hard time ignoring the things Erin Sinclair made him feel.

CHAPTER EIGHT

They'd had a good time and when they finished crabbing, dusk was settling in around them. As he and Erin headed toward town, she introduced him to the two other couples who were staying the night at the B&B. Erin invited them to join her family, but they weren't really crabbers and were going to a restaurant for dinner. So, it was only him who was joining the family. He and Erin walked down the sidewalk to Bake My Day. Adam had picked up Rosie and they got in the backseat of the truck to make the trip to Erin's parents' home.

"My goodness, it feels good to sit down." Rosie settled into the front seat. She turned to smile at them. "It was a really busy day. Everyone was here having such a good time, and we could barely keep muffins stocked, they were ordering so many. Sunset Bay has been very good to me and my business." Rosie smiled at him. "I hope you enjoyed the day. I mean, it was a lovely day and I heard from a little birdie that dropped in that you had ventured out from writing and joined the family."

"I did. It was fun."

"Great. You know, you have a not-so-secret admirer in Lila. She is an adoring fan of yours and spent the afternoon here with her foot propped up. She sang your praises all afternoon and told everyone you had saved her and were down at the water's edge crabbing. I'm surprised you didn't have people hunting you down. I swear, if you had books in there, you could have had your own little book signing."

Erin grinned at him and Adam had laughed as he drove out of the parking lot. "I'm glad to say no one approached me."

"Good. I tried to let them know you were here relaxing and trying to be incognito but that you'd had to come out of hiding to rescue Lila. They all thought that was super sweet and that they wouldn't bother you. But I bet you had a lot of photos taken of you from a distance."

"He did," Erin said. "I caught several taking shots of him."

He had seen a few but had grown so used to the photos that he barely gave it a thought.

"Do you jog?"

He wondered why Rosie was asking. "I have tended to do my share of it. I just didn't do it this morning. Why?"

"Well, let's just say that Lila's friends, Birdie, Doreen, and Mami came in and Mami's obsession is to watch men jogging." Rosie giggled. "She likes it best if they jog shirtless. So, if you're out jogging and you see this rather statuesque lady with a huge smile following you, tracking you or tripping you so she can get close to you, then that's Mami. She's actually nice, but she does have a way about her. Do you jog without your shirt on?"

He laughed at the audaciousness of it all. "No, I'm not one who jogs with my shirt off. And after that description, I'll make sure and keep it on."

"You will highly disappoint her. But that's probably a really good idea. She saw Adam without his shirt on one time… or maybe it was Birdie who saw him. But then, they tracked him often, trying to find where he was jogging so they could watch him. He had adoring fans—well, he still does—but they can always use more friends, so just be careful. If you see her coming, you can stop and say hi or, if you're not brave enough, you can turn around and run very fast the opposite way."

What had he gotten himself into?

Adam laughed. "They're not as bad as she puts on. They didn't tackle me or anything. They're good gals. But yeah, they're a little, well, let's just say they take a little getting used to. But you'll love 'em."

"Okay, I'm taking your word for it, Adam."

Erin chuckled. "You know, if you wrote those romances, you'd have the perfect group to put in there, they are the perfect little group of meddling ladies. They'd fit the bill. You wouldn't even have to make them up—I mean, they're there. You could just sit there and watch how they act. So, you should think about that. I mean, who knows? You could be a great romance writer."

Rosie giggled from the front seat and Adam groaned.

He just looked at Erin. *What was she doing?*

"I think you're pulling my leg. But when I meet these ladies, I have a feeling I'm going to get what you're saying."

"Well, you know, I think from what I've heard, authors tend to see people and create characters in their mind instantly. I think they're perfect, so I'm just saying…"

If she knew that he had already put Lila in his book, she might not be agreeable. He did have a little bit of a different humor and, obviously, it wasn't romance in his books.

They arrived at the house not too far down the main street and one street over. It was a pretty house—

a lot of shrubbery and palm trees. He liked it. It was very homey. When they entered the house with the big crowd of people before them and after them, then went out on the back deck and he saw the view, he really liked it. These people had a wonderful place. It was hard to tell from where they had been driving on the road, but the house was on a curve and it backed up to the water.

She had a big family and lots of friends. What Erin had neglected to tell him was that there was going to be more than just her family there. So, the evening went well except that he spent most of it answering questions from people who had heard down at Bake My Day that he was in town. When he finally made his escape from what seemed like the majority of people being Erin's mother and father's friends, he found her brothers outside around a grill. They were grilling up all kinds of good-looking food.

"You made it out alive, I see." Tate grimaced.

Brad grinned. "We thought we'd warn you, but then we decided we better not because it would really upset Mom and Dad if they hadn't been able to share you with their friends. Plus, we figured if you were here, it'd take the heat off us. Ever since Mom got the bee in her hat to start marrying all her kids off and pushing grandkids on us, we've been a little bit wary about being around her too much. Thankfully, Adam helped us out by marrying Rosie. But, I can see it in Mom's eyes—she's still got the itch. And Lulu and I, well, we decided that we're committed, but we haven't set a date yet. Not yet. Lulu's a little uncomfortable with that, so I'm giving her space. Still, it is nice not to have any heat tonight."

"Glad I could help," Nash said, dryly.

Tate's eyes danced with mirth. "Yeah, and I guess I can personally thank you because I'm only here for the week and then I head out again, but I didn't want to feel my mom breathing down my neck on trying to fix me up. Not happening. I'm not ready for that. These two surprised me. I thought it was going to be Jonah there who was going to be the first one hitched. And look at him, he's still sitting over there, free and easy, and these two have gone and found the women of their dreams. Anyway, you might want to watch your back because I figure Mom is about to concentrate on Erin. You might want to run the next time you get an invite to come over here. By that time, I'll be out of town, so thanks for taking the heat tonight."

He stared at these three guys, four when Jonah stood up from where he sat talking on the phone and then walked over with a grin on his face. "I guess they told you. Thank you very much."

"Yeah, they told me. I was thinking Sunset Bay was a really nice place and now I'm beginning to wonder. Do I have a target on my back or something? Y'all throwing me to the... well, I'd say wolves, but we're talking about your mother."

All the brothers laughed, made several different faces—grimaces, eyebrow waves, wide eyes—all of them saying that he had probably hit the mark in what he was saying. He wondered... "Does Erin know about this?"

The guys all looked at one another and then Brad shrugged. "I think she's fearing for her life. But you know, you are her guest, so there was no way she was going to tell you not to come."

Well, I'll be. He wanted to go back and pack his bags, but then again, he knew what he needed to do was stay here and let the words keep flowing. He knew he needed to be very cautious. He was going to start feeling as though he had to watch everything he said and everywhere he went. He thought he could be inconspicuous here, but it was becoming a little out of hand.

"So how is that hunk of man you have living down there at your B&B doing?" Mami asked the morning that Erin stopped in for more muffins for the B&B.

"Mami, he's fine. He's working hard up there in his room. I hardly see him." It was true. After the party at her parents, he'd told her he'd had a good time. He'd headed up the stairs to his room, then turned and told her that he needed to work all day the next day and would have to put the boat ride off. She had barely seen him since.

Birdie, a wiry lady who had no filters, spoke her mind. "What do you mean you haven't seen him? You two are the only ones living in that big old house, aren't you?"

"Yes, we are, but it's a big house and he wants his space. So, I have my private quarters and the garage where I'm sanding and staining furniture so I stay out of his way. I keep things in the refrigerator for him and I set things out for him, and then I go work on my projects during the day. I am not hovering." Even after he had assured her while they were crabbing that her hovering hadn't been the problem but his attitude had, she still hadn't changed the way she was giving him his space. Especially after he'd canceled the boat ride. She assumed he'd had a change of heart…as in probably heard her mother's over the top need to marry off her children. What had she been thinking, taking him anywhere near her mother?

Lila huffed. "Well, that's not real hospitable. You want to make sure he's comfortable and that he has everything he needs. The poor dear, we don't want him going away from Sunset Bay thinking we're just terrible people. That's really not like you, Erin. You're a good hostess. And like Mami said, he is one hunky fella."

"Lila, you know good and well that I would never neglect my guest. This is what he asked for and I'm honoring that. Believe me, I was not okay with it at first." To be honest, she was starting to be bothered by it again. She'd thought at the crab festival that there was a connection between them. She'd had one moment when she'd thought he wanted to kiss her. And when he hadn't, she'd been so disappointed. There had also been a moment when she thought he was going to reveal something about himself that was important. But he hadn't. She'd been disappointed in that, also but then the canceled boat ride—that had hit hard. She had really been looking forward to spending time on the water with him.

"I'm not going to bother him. I think he was having writer's block when he arrived and he was very grouchy. But suddenly he's not having it anymore. And I think he's happy about that."

It was true and she told herself it wasn't personal. That he wasn't hiding from her because of her mother's matchmaking overtures.

"Writer's block?" Mami gasped. "I bet that's why they pushed the release date of his new book back for a year."

"A year?" She stared at Mami who nodded.

"Yes," Lila said. "He usually releases one book a year and so those of us who read him are a little frustrated about that."

"I think something happened," Doreen said, softly. "I think he had a personal issue."

Everyone looked at her.

"What?" Erin asked, suddenly alert. *It fit.*

"Did you read something?" Mami asked.

"Well…no," Doreen hesitated, bringing her hands together on the table as she thought about her next words. "I have to admit that I would love to *meet* him. But I did see him that very first day. I was coming out of the pharmacy. I had gone in there and picked up some chamomile tea. You know, it helps me sleep at night. And I just stopped and gawked as he was passing by. He was on the phone with someone and preoccupied. I couldn't believe it was really him! I mean, I see him in his advertisements for his books.

And you know, he talks in those advertisements, and he's got such a very nice voice, so deep and rich. But to hear him in person, well, I was in heaven. He smiled at me, distracted as he was, he smiled, and I tell you I felt a little faint. I really, really did. He continued what he was saying and kept on walking, and I got my second wind and I tell you I almost chased him down just to keep listening to that amazing voice of his. But I'm so clumsy I would have probably tripped over my feet and fallen flat on my face. That would not have been good at all." She took a deep breath.

Everybody looked at one another because they all knew what she said was true. Doreen was a little top heavy because she was so very well endowed in the breast region and so short and, well, she didn't have a whole lot of coordination. But if Doreen had fallen, she might have tripped him and he might have fallen on Doreen. The thought suddenly had Erin thinking about tripping in front of Nash— *Halt. Stop. What are you thinking?*

She had had the man on her mind. She hadn't been sleeping well. She slept in the room two floors below him. She thought about him constantly. It was ridiculous, and she couldn't tell anybody that. If it got out to anybody, *anybody*, that she was distracted and flustered by the man, she would never live it down. Never. It was top secret. Her lips were sealed. But, the truth was, she had him on her mind. She laid in bed at night, twiddling her thumbs and staring at the ceiling, wondering whether he was still up there pounding those keys. Or whether he was sleeping. Or whether he was sitting out on the balcony, watching the moonlight. Sometimes she would sit on her patio below his balcony and watch the moonlight, but not since he had arrived because she didn't want to make a noise while he was out there and be accused of disturbing him.

"Doreen," Birdie snapped. "That was a fun story but what did it have to do with what we were talking about? You know, when you said you thought he might have had a personal issue?"

Lila and Mami nodded.

Doreen waved a hand and looked embarrassed. "I got carried away. Sorry. He was talking on the phone.

And he told whoever was on the other end that yes, he was making peace with his grief."

Erin's heart clutched and all eyes were on Doreen.

"You're sure that's what you heard?" Lila asked.

As Doreen nodded, her sweet face full of worry, Erin placed a hand on her shoulder. "Thanks for telling us." She felt terrible. *Was he grieving someone?* His words played through her thoughts: *In this past year, I've had more bad days than good.*

It all made sense to her. He had come here with no words and worried about the fact that he wasn't producing them. Her heart squeezed as she felt for him. He was a solitary man; even if she hadn't read that, she knew it. He had no roots, at least none she had read about or heard about. But something had happened that made him have writer's block or as he called it, no words. *Who had he lost?* Because she sensed that this was it. And he had almost told her at the festival. Her heart thundered at this revelation. And suddenly, she wanted to be the person he could talk to. Whoever he'd been discussing it with on the phone wasn't here. But she was.

"Are you okay?" Mami asked.

She roused from her thoughts to find them all staring at her with expectant eyes. She bit her lip and slid a glance at the counter and saw that Rosie was also watching her. "I'm fine. Like I said, ladies, when you see him, please try to give him his space. And believe me, I am making sure he has everything he needs while staying at the B&B. If he wants it, he knows exactly where to find it."

At her words, Rosie giggled, Lila got a very mischievous look on her face, Mami hitched a brow, Doreen just looked embarrassed, and Birdie grinned from ear to ear.

"Okay, so what is that all about?"

Birdie said, "Well, you said it: he has everything there he might want and if he needs something, he knows where to find it. So maybe he might want to have a conversation with a pretty blonde who is his hostess. Or maybe he might want to come downstairs and have dinner with the pretty blonde who is his hostess. Girl, don't you pass up this opportunity of a lifetime. Not every female in the world gets the opportunity to spend alone time with one of the most famous, gorgeous adventure and intrigue novelists of our time. And eligible bachelor. I would be making the most of it."

Lila winked at her. "I know your mama didn't raise a fool. And I can see that there's interest in your eyes. How do I know this? Because you're a female and you're of the right age and, well, the day that he helped me up here with my ankle, I saw sparks and you know I did. So, I think you need to get out some romantic candles and invite him downstairs for a little rendezvous. Make one of those really nice meals you know how to make."

She held her hand up. "Okay, back it up, ladies. This is getting out of hand. I'm his hostess. I'm not auditioning for his girlfriend."

Mami huffed. "Well, you should be. What is wrong with you?"

She just let out a long sigh and shook her head. "Okay, I'm not answering that. I'm out of here. Thanks for the warning, ladies. Talk to you later, or maybe if I see you coming, maybe I won't."

CHAPTER NINE

By mid-week on his second week in Sunset Bay, Nash had forced himself to avoid his beautiful hostess as much as possible. After the conversation he'd had with her brothers at the party, he'd decided taking her boating was not a good idea. He didn't need anyone getting ideas about matchmaking. He stayed in his room, worked, and only after he heard her moving around in the garden below him did he venture down for a snack. She continued to silently place a carafe of coffee and pitcher of water next to his door, so that enabled him not to have to be desperate for anything.

Even after the time they'd spent at the festival and at her parents' home getting to know each other a little better, she was still giving him his space. He was glad because it was working. He was getting a lot of work done.

He had his rough draft going really, really well. He still had to do a lot of work on it, but he was pleased with what was happening to it. His little female villain he had put into the book, he didn't figure anyone would figure out that she was the villain until it was too late, just like his characters.

He was in the kitchen now, pulling the platter of baked chicken, cheese, grapes, and a cheese ball and crackers from the refrigerator. There was a note at the top of it that said, *Enjoy, Nash.* Oh, he was. She was good. She had figured out what he liked to eat when he was writing. He liked finger foods. He could snack on it, and it wasn't too heavy, and it was protein. It didn't make him sleepy. It kept his energy up. The thing about those wonderful-tasting muffins that she had first tried to hoist on him—yeah, they were delicious, but they were carbohydrates and could kill his energy. But sometimes she would surprise him with small bowls of caramel corn, and despite the carbs, he enjoyed every bite.

He was about to take the plate up to his room when his gaze was drawn down the short hallway to her door. A week of solitude was enough, and he decided it was time to at least tell Erin that she was doing good. He had thought about her a lot, thought of wanting to kiss her, and that had kept him holed up and doing his work. He didn't need to tempt himself too much. He set the platter on the table and walked through the butler's pantry to the door that he knew led to her chambers.

Standing there momentarily, trying to talk himself out of what he was about to do, he tapped on the door and waited. In a moment, the door opened. She wore a pair of yoga pants and a tank top, and her hair was pulled back in a ponytail.

"Nash, hello. Is something wrong? Do I need to get something for you?"

He just stared at her. She was like a breath of fresh air. He had been holed up too long. He had forgotten what a woman looked like, because this one was beautiful. "No… I've gotten more words written than I've gotten in a long time. This place is working for me in ways I never thought possible. I might have to rent indefinitely at this point." He smiled at her stunned expression. "I'm kidding. Don't be scared."

"Oh no, I wasn't. I'm happy."

"Good. I was wondering if you would come join me for dinner. I needed a break and…don't pass out or anything but I wanted company."

She looked stunned and she blinked hard before recovering. She crossed her arms and leaned against the doorframe. A smile tickled the corners of her mouth. "Really? The recluse needs company?"

He smiled at her. "Your company. That roasted chicken platter you made me is big enough for a football team. So I thought we could share."

He had taken her completely by surprise.

"I've been doing yoga. I'm a little sweaty."

"I think you're fine." *In more ways than one.*

She glanced down at herself and then back up. "Well, okay, sure."

She moved into the hallway, and he let her pass, then followed her through the butler's pantry and into the kitchen. Suddenly, the room seemed really, really small and he didn't mind that at all. She spun to find him standing right behind her, and he automatically reached out and grabbed her arms to steady her. Or, maybe he used that as an excuse to touch her. Her skin was soft and toned, and his fingers tightened with the need to pull her into his arms. He leaned forward with a sudden desire to kiss her startled lips. He caught himself before it was too late. "Don't…don't trip or anything. I might have to rescue you."

She laughed, jumpy and a bit shaky as her beautiful eyes held his. "Yes. No, I mean. I wouldn't want you to have to do that, but…do you drink wine? I can get a bottle out of the pantry."

"Actually, I don't drink, but thanks for asking. Must be the good hostess in you."

Her tongue moistened her lips and she breathed a deep, noticeable breath. "Well, like I said, I do try! We'll have tea. I have plenty of iced tea."

He tucked his fingers into his pockets, to help

keep him from reaching for her. He'd had her on his mind but blocked her out as he wrote. But now, seeing her standing here so close, he wondered how he'd do that now. "That sounds perfect."

"So, why did you decide to write intrigue and adventure? They are two different genres and you are good at both. I know, I know—I said I don't read it, but I couldn't help myself. I've been reading one of your stories every night before I go to bed. You know, you scared me half to death."

He laughed. "No way. I don't write stuff that scares people that bad."

"Yes, you do. Like I said, I read romance. I don't read thrillers or suspense."

"Obviously not if the book scared you that much. I'm going to have to toughen you up."

She laughed this time. "I still just have a little bit left and I'm kind of scared to read it because I just don't know what's going to happen to the poor guy down in that hole. And I have this fear that you're going to kill off the hero or the heroine."

"Oh, you're reading *Hour Glass*! That was kind of intriguing down in that cave. I won't tell you the ending, but it's not going to be a terrible ending."

"Is she going to get rescued?"

"Yes, and the bad guy is going to get justice in a very just way."

"Well, he could fall into a dark hole in the ground in the cave and that would suit me just fine, traumatizing her like that."

He just smiled. "I'm not going to give away the ending, just help you to relax a little bit."

"Really? Again, to remind you, there's a huge market out there of romance readers. They're voracious. They love romance. You throw in some of those hunky detectives that you have in your books—yes, I've read blurbs—and have a love brew between your protagonist and the woman and you could get readers like me to read you."

"And alienate my loyal readership."

"If you did it right, maybe you could keep both audiences."

"I don't think so."

"Too bad. If you tweaked your guys a touch, they would be wonderful heroes. They could fall in love, they could solve mysteries, they could save the heroine, and I bet that your books could sell more than the millions and millions that they sell now."

He grinned so big that she almost dropped her fork. *Goodness, the man was amazing.* She needed to concentrate on her food, not that smile or that captivating look in his eyes that told her that he might be…well, she didn't want to think about what he might be thinking about. It was too intriguing. He was her guest. Nothing more.

"I'm not sure how it would turn out with me writing a romance, I already told you that. I'm not the most romantic kind of fellow. I don't even know what I would put in those kinds of books."

"You don't have to say it like it's a dirty word or a horrible thing. You invited me to dinner tonight. This is..." She paused, realizing she was about to say this meal was romantic. "I mean, oh my goodness, I was going to say," she laughed nervously, "that this…"

"Are you trying to say this is classified as a romantic dinner?" He surveyed the meal skeptically.

She ran a nervous hand through her blonde hair and didn't answer.

"Well, is it?" he urged.

"Not technically. It's just two of us sitting here having a meal that I made, but it's *kind* of romantic if you wrote the scene in a book…your hero, could have left her in her room and ate alone. Nothing romantic about that. But, he instead decides to invite the heroine to eat with him. And there is the start…" What was she doing?

"Oh, I see." He grinned and crossed his arms and watched her and she knew he knew she was in a corner. "Let's say I was going to write this in a book. How would I make it more romantic? You know, for the ladies?"

He was incorrigible. She could only play along. "If you really wanted to make it romantic, he would go into the pantry first and get a tablecloth, a couple of candlesticks and matches, then set the table. *Or better yet*, you, I mean your hero, would have set it up out on the deck, with the evening moonlight glowing and the birds and crickets singing. He would have the candles flaming and then he would knock on her door and invite her to join you, I mean him." She chuckled as she got a picture in her mind of flames going wild.

"What's so funny? I thought you were painting a pretty good picture myself. I really messed up by not having candlesticks flaming while the birds and crickets serenade."

She laughed. "The 'candles flaming'—that kind of got me tickled. If you wanted it to be a romantic comedy when the heroine comes outside, the candlesticks would be flaming, the tablecloth would be on fire, and we'd have to call Brad and his crew to put the fire out and rescue the hero and heroine. *Or*, if you really want to make it romantic, he could rescue her instead of Brad. That would work."

Nash rubbed his jaw and his eyes crinkled around the edges. "Since you're so good at this, we could write a story together. That's what we could do while I'm here—we could write an intriguing romance or a compelling romantic comedy. Maybe that's how it would work out."

They smiled and stared at each other. He was funny, and she was enjoying herself way too much. "I don't know about me helping you write it, but I think you could do it. If anyone could create a new genre, you could."

"No, no—if I did that, you'd have to help me. I'll ask my agent about it tomorrow. She'll check it out and get back to me about what the market can stand."

"You're kidding, right?"

"No, I'm not. You keep mentioning it and so did the ladies the other night. I'm starting to think that maybe I am missing out on a market. Grumpy old me, you know, I'm stuck in a rut. Maybe I could throw a romance in the mix and create a new and improved Nash Bond."

She laughed. "Sure. That sounds like the words of a movie trailer. The new and improved *Nash Bond.* Sounds like a blockbuster hit."

"See? It could be Nash Bond and Erin Sinclair." He used his hand to sweep, as if showing a banner with their names on it.

She giggled. "My name just does not have the same sound as Nash Bond. Is that really your name?"

His dark eyes twinkled or glittered dangerously. Dangerously as in dangerous to her heart.

"It actually is my real name. My adoptive dad gave me that name," he said, with a tenderness in his voice and his eyes shadowed.

His adoptive dad. Her pulse increased. She'd read that he'd been adopted somewhere but not much else had been said. *Could he have died? Could this be who Doreen overheard him talking about grieving?* Because he'd looked so sad suddenly.

"He picked a good one." It was all she knew to say at this point.

"I wanted a new name when he adopted me. I wanted his last name but I also wanted a new first name. I didn't want my old name."

Her heart tugged at the look that came into his eyes as they met hers. She wanted to know everything about him. And this was something she didn't think anyone knew. "Why?" she asked quietly.

He didn't answer at first, and she thought he was

lost in the past for a moment as he considered his words.

"He was my new father, the only father I ever want to claim. So, I asked him to give me a name like any father would do when their son was born. Because to me, the day he rescued me and became my mentor was the day that I started to live again. The day he adopted me was the best day of my life. He understood, and he gave me a name that he thought would sell books since he knew that was what I dreamed of doing."

"It is a great name. Intriguing," she offered. She felt for him deeply. *He'd needed rescuing.*

"I'm sure he's proud of you."

She sensed deep sorrow in him. From what he'd told her about his past and his adoptive father it was easy to piece together the fact that he had been a wonderful man. Looking at Nash, knowing he'd been in a very dark place as a child, Erin loved this father who had been Nash's rescuer. She wished she could tell him.

"Yes."

They nibbled food in silence for a few moments, both lost in thoughts and at last she couldn't help but ask, "He knew you were going to be a writer?"

He toyed with his chicken, pushing it around with his fork, and then slid a sly look toward her. "Yes, but he didn't know I was going to be a writer of romantic, suspense comedy or whatever genre we're going to name it. But he knew I was going to be some kind of writer, because I wrote everything down. It was my escape. I started writing when I was about five, the stories were childish but I'd create them, write them down on anything I could write on. When I met Gerald, I started keeping the pages. He taught me that anything I wrote down was worth keeping. Worth remembering and worth sharing. He taught me that I was worth cultivating and encouraging."

Her heart clutched as they stared at each other for the longest moment.

"He died a little over a year ago."

The words were calm, but she heard a river of pain flowing below the surface. She had known he was dead. Had felt it and now she wanted so badly to comfort him. Following her heart, she covered his hand with hers. "I'm sorry. So, so sorry. I wish I had known him."

Emotion filled his eyes and after a moment, he turned his hand so that he held hers. "Thank you. He was worth knowing."

"From what you've told me, I completely agree. What was his name?"

"Gerald Bond. And everyone who came in contact with him was better for it. I try to write stories that elevate the type of man he was. I like to write stories where goodness overcomes darkness, because Gerald Bond taught me that through his words and through his actions that's what he did in my life. He was my hero."

And now she understood.

His thumb made small strokes along her thumb. "I miss him."

Her heart broke, and she thought of her own dad and how grateful she was for his love and to still have him in her life. Unable to stop herself, she touched his cheek with her free hand. Cupped his bristly jaw. "You loved him. You're still grieving him and that's why your words dried up isn't it? It's understandable."

He nodded. "You have been looking in my head, it seems."

"I'm glad you opened a window and let me in. I've felt like something had happened to you."

She wanted to know why he had been on the streets in the first place but he would tell her that when he was ready. If he wanted to. Looking at him, all she wanted to do in that moment was to be there for him.

"It's life. I haven't shared any of that with anyone." Counselors knew it from when he was young. He didn't share anything about the trauma he lived through as a child.

"I'm glad you felt you could share it with me. I'm so sorry you went through something so terrible you had to be rescued. I can't imagine."

He didn't retell the story of his alcoholic father and his drug addict mother or the abuses he suffered. He didn't tell anyone about life on the streets until Gerald came into his life and took him in. It was too private, too painful. People knew he had a hard background, but that was it. That was all he'd ever divulged and no one had dug deep enough to find out more. But he'd opened completely up to Erin as they sat at the non-candle lit, non-romantic dinner…the best dinner he had in a very long time because it was shared with Erin and made by her too. He liked her. Was drawn to her like he'd never been drawn to anyone.

"My life with my dad was good. They don't come any better than Gerald Bond." He wanted to pull Erin into his arms and forget about his past and look…toward the future. And that was something he had never felt before.

He didn't even know if he could do a relationship. He'd never let anyone in and dating never moved into relationship status. Things always fell apart for him before too long and he moved on. Took total blame for it. He didn't know that he would bring Erin into something like that—she was too good, too nice and he didn't want to take a chance of hurting her. Her life was too perfect. He was not sure how someone like him, who was moody and grumpy and used to getting his own way, and was aloof and who sometimes, still, had nightmares…no, he wouldn't bring that into her perfect life.

What was he thinking, anyway? Where had all this come from?

"I better go up and work now. Thanks for the good meal." He stood and picked up his plate. She looked a little bit stunned by his sudden decision. Understandable, considering they had just been having a conversation and now he was heading to his room without even ending the conversation. And this was why he was no good with relationships…it was all about him.

But he needed to write; the grip of the book was on him suddenly and he needed to get the words on paper. And things were getting too personal.

He paused at the door. "I'm sorry. I get things on my mind and I get blunt like that." Another reason he wouldn't be good at a relationship. "I really enjoyed this, but I need to go write, now." He held his plate, ready to place it in the sink.

"Yes, of course. You go write. I'll clean this up.

Thanks for inviting me. And Nash, thank you for sharing about your dad with me. I feel honored to know about him and how he loved you. And you loved him."

He hesitated, his heart thundering.

"Really," she said, softly, placing her hand on his holding the plate. "I'll get this."

His skin where her skin touched him burned. He tried to let go of the plate, but if he let go of the plate, it would mean her hand wouldn't be touching his anymore.

She smiled up at him. "You came here to write, so go. I've got this."

He loved her smile. It made him long for things…

The best thing he could do for her was to walk away. His gaze dropped to her lips and he yanked them back up and nodded. "Thanks." He turned and got himself up those stairs to his room as fast as his long legs would carry him.

CHAPTER TEN

The next morning, after the dinner that shouldn't have been, Erin left orange juice in the refrigerator and muffins in the muffin holder and left the house early, needing space. She left a little note that said she would return mid-morning. Not that he cared whether she was there or not; still, she was the proprietor of the Inn at Sunset Bay and felt obligated to leave the message. She particularly wanted him to know this considering it would be her changing his sheets today since her cleaning lady had called in sick. Of all the days to do that—now she would be responsible for knocking on his door and disturbing him.

She'd left the note, so he could get out of his room for the afternoon for an hour and then come back. She had left him in control.

She, on the other hand, was not in control. She hadn't slept at all. All she could do was think about the guy. She went from being upset to being aggravated. Nash was the one who had brought up his past. She thought about that as she made her way to Bake My Day. She needed to see Rosie's happy, sunny smile. Rosie—always in a good spirit, always willing to help someone have a good day. And boy did she need one.

The moment she walked in the door and saw how busy it was, she stopped right there at the door and just stared. There were people everywhere. It was rush hour—what had she been thinking? Rosie was filling orders, smiling and laughing and lifting spirits as she worked. The line of people waiting didn't even mind as she kept them all smiling. All the tables were very nearly full too.

This was no time to try talk to Rosie.

She froze in the door, her stomach sinking. Rosie saw her, smiled across the room at her. "Erin, come over here." Feeling hopeful she weaved her way through the tables and moved to the end of the counter.

"Gigi, can you take over for me right here, please?" she asked her barista.

"Sure can." Gigi took her place, shooting Erin a worried look.

"Gigi will take great care of all of you," she said with a big smile and then came to the end of the counter. "Erin, you look…distraught. Is everything okay?"

Of course, Rosie had a way of seeing through people's expressions. "It's not my best day. I thought maybe a cup of your coffee and one of your muffins would help."

Rosie cocked her head to one side. "You have a batch of my muffins at your B&B, so I'm thinking that if that's what you really came here for, you or that handsome tenant of yours must have really gorged on muffins last night."

Erin inhaled and let out a long sigh. Her shoulders

slumped. "Okay, in truth, I came to chat. I need someone to help me not go crazy, but you are swamped. I couldn't even dream of taking you away from this."

Rosie didn't even hesitate. "Gigi, I have to step out for a few minutes." Then, she reached over to the coffee machine, poured a cup of coffee to go, placed a lid on it and handed it to Erin. "Let's go."

Erin was not in the mood to argue with her. "Thank you. I feel really silly about doing this."

Rosie laced her arm through Erin's and propelled them down the sidewalk toward the ocean. "Nonsense. No time to feel silly. When you have a problem, it's good to talk about it. And Erin, I don't know if you've noticed this, but you aren't one to talk about your problems very often. Therefore, when you show up at my bakery with that look on your face of complete confusion and dismay, girl, I'm with you. We're going to talk and we are going to see what we can do about whatever is bothering you. I'm not passing that up."

Erin didn't talk about her problems often to anyone. Her family hadn't known how important Nash

Bond's stay was for her. They didn't know that her dream of a B&B had slowly turned into a stress-inducing fight to keep her head above water. She hadn't been able to admit it to anyone, and she still couldn't.

Erin had had high hopes that she would open her B&B—it was just so beautiful, though she still had a couple of rooms to finish, the rest of it was in great shape. However, the vision and the dream of people flocking to her place to relax for the weekend or have a romantic honeymoon, wasn't happening. The growth was slower than she'd projected and though she wasn't advertising for a full house yet, the bookings just weren't there for even the rooms she had available.

And she needed them. And then there was Nash, riding in on his white stallion, though he didn't realize he was riding in on a white stallion to save the day. Nor did he probably care. But, for her, that was exactly what had happened when she got that call that *the* Nash Bond was coming to stay at her B&B. She had believed a good review could help her Inn at Sunset Bay.

She had no idea that his being here was going to tie her into knots.

Last night she had thought they had had a connection. He'd invited her to eat with him and then he'd opened up about his past, and she knew that was unusual for him. She'd thought that had meant something. And then he had gone from being nice and teasing and inviting her to dinner and then to just a complete shutdown.

"Hello," Rosie said and waved a hand in front of her eyes. "You just checked out on me."

Erin paused to stare across the sand at the topaz ocean. She rubbed her forehead as she watched the seagulls dipping and diving toward the water. "Okay, Nash is driving me crazy."

"Really? Is that crazy in a good way, or crazy in a bad way? Is he doing something he shouldn't be doing? I mean, you two are in that house alone. Do I need to send your brothers over there?"

Erin laughed. "No, no, nothing like that. He's a perfect gentleman. He still holes up most of the time. I mean, I'm thinking about him all the time, and though

I don't spend that much time with him, I want to." There, she admitted it to Rosie and to herself.

"I assumed that. When you look at him, you might not want to do this, but your eyes light up and you get all nervous. Erin, in the time that I've been here and come to know you…that's not you. I've never really seen you nervous. So, I have found that Nash Bond being here is very interesting in a very nice way." She chuckled. "He shakes you up."

"Rosie, it's not funny."

Rosie smiled. "Oh yes, it is. You were the one talking about those butterflies that you thought were dead. Remember?"

"Well, they're not dead. They are very much alive and well, whether I want them to be or not."

Frustration drove her across the sand to the water's edge. When they reached it, Rosie picked up a rock and threw it into the water. "I love this place. I love it so much. I can honestly tell you that I think that Nash's agent was brilliant bringing him here. I looked at the pictures on the website of that room, and you have that one shot of the balcony, and then you have the shot from the balcony, the one that overlooks the shops below, and right past them you can see the boardwalk going into the water. It's a beautiful shot. It's very peaceful and pleasant and alluring. That shot is what got him here. You took that, didn't you?"

"Well, no, I didn't take it. I had Cassie take professional shots for me for the website. My sister is very talented. I think it's so beautiful and I wasn't sure if my shot would be professional enough."

Now that she thought about it, she knew that was it, though. It was a lovely shot, and sitting on that balcony and just being in your own little world and still getting to be able to see that picturesque view was just lovely. She envisioned him being up there, just dreaming away and concocting his stories. She tried to think about that rather than thinking about him being in the honeymoon suite alone. Because, yes, that thought had also come into her mind more nights than she cared to think about. Those were very sleepless nights. *No thinking about that.* She was not in the market for a honeymoon suite anytime soon, and she had repeated that mantra and repeated that mantra over and over again in her head.

"Erin, what about him scares you?" Rosie's question was right on target.

"Writing is his life. He has no roots that hold him down, and, I think he likes it that way. He came here needing to soothe his soul." She didn't elaborate on that but knew after last night that it was true. "But I have no doubt that when he's finished with his time here…he will leave." *And take my heart with him, if I'm not careful.*

"Erin, as your friend, please don't close your heart off. Love can overcome great obstacles. He might not leave. Yes, you could get hurt. But if you don't take a risk, won't you always wonder what might have been if you'd just given it a fair chance?"

Twenty minutes later, Erin was still mulling over Rosie's words as she climbed the stairs to Nash's room. She'd scooped up the new linens from the housekeeping room just below his room and headed up. She wasn't sure whether he was there or not. She had purposefully gone to her patio below his balcony and listened for any signs that he was in his room. The fact that she didn't hear him pounding out words on his computer hopefully told her that the man had read her note and gone out to give her the hour alone in his room to clean.

She hesitated at the door and then tapped lightly. She really didn't want to run into him today. "Hello," she called softly. Hearing nothing, she pushed open the door and walked silently into the room. "Hello," she called. The curtains were drawn and the room was dimly lit as she glanced over to the very rumpled bed. Nash was obviously a restless sleeper. Which fit everything she knew about him. Realizing he wasn't here she moved across the suite and into the slightly ajar door to the bathroom.

The moment she entered the bathroom the moist heat from a recent shower enveloped her. Alert, she spun toward the shower just as the door opened and Nash stepped out of the steaming enclosure.

She gasped and dropped the armload of towels and sheets she'd been carrying. Thankfully, he had a towel draped loosely around his hips. She gaped at him. Took in all the damp muscles and far too much skin for her to process at one time. The man was a writer, but he obviously worked out at some point in time, because surely to goodness, God hadn't just graced him with that body for no reason or without any work.

"Erin, what are you doing in here?" He looked completely unfazed.

At his question, everything that had been in slow motion clicked and she dropped to the floor, scrambling to pick up the linens. Anything other than staring at him.

"I left you a note downstairs. I *told* you I'd be in the room at this time. I knocked on the door and no one answered. *I thought you were gone.*" She was rambling—oh, she was rambling. "I'm sorry. I called out. No one answered. I didn't have any idea."

He knelt beside her. She didn't need him beside her, bringing those damp muscles closer to her. She lifted her eyes. His dark hair curled at his nape and that rebellious lock of dark hair teased her fingers as it hung there on his forehead. His eyes danced. And a grin splashed across his face. "This isn't funny, Nash."

"It's okay, Erin. If you had walked in a second sooner, it might not have been. I was up writing all night and I slept in this morning, so I didn't see your note. I honestly just woke up a few minutes ago."

He put his hand on hers and thankfully kept one hand tightly on his towel. "Calm down. It's fine. Look at me, Erin."

Oh, she was looking at him all right. "This is not all right. It's so unprofessional."

"Come on. Can you stop with all that professional stuff? We are long past you having to worry about if I'm enjoying my stay or you messing up my stay. Just relax. Everything is fine. Now, if you give me a minute, I'll get dressed and I'll go for a walk to clear my head while you do your thing. It's been a very productive night for me, and I'm ready to get out and explore a little bit."

She stared at him, so off-centered she was afraid she might fall over and fought off wanting to throw herself at him. *It had been a productive night for him while she had gotten no sleep after their dinner last night and his abrupt exit?* She fought back the temptation to snap at him, but that would be very unprofessional.

"Okay then. I'll go get fresh towels and give you a few minutes. Just leave the door open when you leave since it's just us and you don't have to worry about anyone else coming in when you leave."

He grinned far too sexily for her own good. *Did he know he was grinning sexily? Drat the man.* She stood, straightened her shoulders, then marched with as much dignity as she could muster from the bathroom to the door, with his chuckles following.

Thirty minutes later, Nash strolled down Main Street in search of a sandwich. But, as he passed Bake My Day, his stomach growled and a craving for a strawberry delight cream cheese muffin and a cup of Bake My Day ground coffee filled his thoughts. Boy, he was turning into a wimp with this sweet addiction that he suddenly had. He had always been a strict protein eater with very little carbs, but being in this town with those muffins, he was starting to find the temptation too great to pass up.

It was nearly two o'clock when he walked in the doors, and the place was quiet. He assumed it did its biggest business in the early morning and mid-morning. He was startled when he walked into the room and was immediately greeted by Lila and her mischievous friends.

"Hello, my handsome rescuer and favorite author," Lila greeted with a big grin on her face.

The ladies sat at the table next to the window and had probably been watching him the whole time he'd been standing outside on the sidewalk contemplating coming inside. He grinned. "Hi, ladies."

They all waved and Lila continued talking. "I have been wanting to see you. I thought you would come by my house to see me sometime and you haven't. Of course, I know you are writing. Come here. Let me buy you a muffin and a coffee."

Mami gave him a sly look that he did not trust. "Pull up a chair and take a load off. You stay up there in that little room too much. We never see you."

Considering he avoided her the few times he'd seen her colorful caftans that she wore, waving in the wind in the distance when he jogged, he knew exactly why she never saw him. From what Erin's brothers had told him about this crafty group, he'd been avoiding all of them.

"By the way, young man," Mami said, giving him a shrewd look. "I saw you jogging the other morning, but you were too far away to reach before you spun and jogged the opposite way. I think you might have been avoiding me on purpose. I don't think you had a shirt on either." She sighed.

Nash had an urge to laugh. She was a plucky lady.

Birdie, tiny but blunt, snapped, "Mami, you and your jogging men. If you would get off your tush and do a little jogging yourself, you might be able to catch your own man. But sitting there on the porch or on the sea wall watching shirtless men jog by is not doing you any good."

Shy Doreen, who was almost as wide in her upper body as she was in the whole length of herself, giggled. The sweet lady had a nice grin, and she was blushing, which Nash thought was endearing. *How many ladies her age still blushed?*

"You ladies need to remember," she said, with a wave of her hand. "He's standing right here. Goodness gracious girls, he can *hear* you."

That made them all laugh, and though he hadn't had the chance to say anything, other than his quick greeting, now he did. "I have to say, I haven't been greeted this way in a long time. And you ladies are exactly the people I was looking for this morning."

Not what he'd been planning but now that he saw them, he knew he did want to visit with them. He purposefully pulled a seat up and sat next to Doreen.

"Lila, how have you been doing? I gather how Mami and Birdie are doing—they seem like they're getting on just like the last time I saw them." That made Doreen and the rest of them laugh again. He winked at Mami, since he was implying that they were just as mischievous and grumpy as they had been the last time he saw them.

Lila grinned at him. "I'm doing great! I can actually walk on my ankle, although Doctor Adam told me to stay off it a little longer. It's just so hard to do. But I am. See, I have it up on the chair right now."

Rosie came over to join the conversation. "She neglected to say that she walked in here and *then* put it up on the chair. I'm not real sure that Adam would think she's following the doctor's orders."

"What he doesn't know won't hurt him," Lila cooed.

"But it could hurt you, so please don't rush it," Rosie said.

"I'll try." Lila sighed.

"Thank you." Rosie looked relieved then studied him. "How are you doing, Nash?"

He saw speculation in her eyes. He was good at reading people—maybe too good. But, that came with being a writer. He studied people—he studied mannerisms, how they looked from one time to another. And Rosie had something on her mind.

"I'm doing really well. I had a very productive evening. I was up most of the night writing. My story is flowing, so I haven't eaten, and as I was walking by I had a craving for one of those muffins—you know, a strawberry one with the cream cheese?"

Rosie laughed. "Great. I'll get you one."

Lila looked delighted. "I knew you would like those! I just love them." She patted her stomach. "I have to do my yoga more, but it's worth it."

Mami eyed his stomach, then brought her gaze to his. "You might need to jog a bit more to make sure that muffin doesn't settle in your midriff." She smiled at him. "It would be a shame if you got a muffin top."

He laughed. "No muffin tops for me, or donuts or whatever else it's called. I'll pound the pavement more, though, if that's what it takes to eat Rosie's muffins."

"Watch yourself, Mami, trying to warn people away from my sweets," Rosie warned, laughter in her voice. "I'll bring the muffin to you right away. I'll bring two since you haven't eaten. And a cup of coffee." It wasn't a question; it was a statement as she turned away and hurried back behind the counter. She smiled as she looked at him over the counter and hitched a shoulder. He knew she was enjoying the sight of him with these rambunctious, not shy ladies.

He was enjoying them too.

"So, ladies, I'm working on my story and I realized that I need a few insights into this little town."

Lila gasped. "Are you using our town as a setting for your book?"

"I'm using it as the setting for a new story idea I'm tossing around in my head while I write my other story, which is coming along well." It was true, but he had not been able to stop thinking about his conversation with Erin the night before. He hadn't been able to stop thinking about Erin at all. But somehow amid the thoughts of her and their conversation and his rude behavior to her, words had come, and they had come quickly. They had flowed from his fingertips to the computer with the ease that they used to come to him. He was in the game again and he knew if things kept going like this, he would be able to supply the book his fans and his publisher were waiting for him to deliver.

But he had that niggling idea in the back of his head that he could try something new, and the ideas were tossing and turning in the back of his mind. And he wanted to explore them. Last night, sitting on the balcony, watching the moon dance on the water, he knew this was something he was going to do.

He had achieved a success that most authors dreamed of. It wasn't something he had to continue to do, and he was at a stage in his life where he realized he could afford to write whatever he wanted. He didn't want to disappoint his fans, but at this point in time, he needed to try something new.

"So, what are you saying?" Mami asked.

"Yes, spit it out," Birdie grunted.

This made him smile.

"I'm just toying with some ideas and you ladies have inspired me."

Doreen looked up at him, her eyes wide, and a hand went to her heart. "You mean you're putting us in a book?" She blushed brilliant burgundy upon this declaration. "I mean, I didn't mean to…"

He smiled. "I'm not putting you in a book, but the way you are, the way you ladies interact and the way you love your town—that's inspiring. And you are inspiring characters in my book, in a good way. Don't worry."

That set them all talking. And by the time Rosie brought his muffins and his coffee, they were glowing.

Lila beamed up at Rosie. "We are going to be in a book. Nash is putting us in a book! Can you believe it?"

He groaned. He had messed up. "Now, Lila, remember I said you *inspired* characterization. It's not you. If and when I write this story, you inspired me to write characters who enjoy life the way you ladies do." *There, maybe that was clearer.* He didn't mention that he'd also based a devious character on the sweet lady that no one would suspect in his current work in progress.

"Well, if I inspire a character, then I'm assuming that it's me."

Mami elbowed Lila. "He said you are inspiring a character, Lila. Take what you can get. And who knows what kind of a character you are inspiring. He didn't say it was a complimentary character. If I were you, I'd mind my Ps and Qs." Mami winked at him and then crossed her arms and dipped her chin. "What kind of a character, may I ask, do I inspire?"

"Boy, are you brave." Birdie snorted.

He grinned and picked up his muffin. "A very bold character. A very nice and bold character."

"That's putting it politely," Birdie said.

"Then that is just fine. I like you, Nash Bond. If you get that book written, I'll buy a dozen of them, even if they're hardbacks. Might buy more than that."

Rosie placed a hand on his shoulder. "Careful, Nash, you might have created monsters."

He chuckled. Maybe he had, but they would be nice monsters.

CHAPTER ELEVEN

Erin was ripping weeds from her flowerbeds with a vengeance when she felt eyes on her.

"So that's how you keep your garden so pretty," Nash said from above her. "You attack the weeds with gusto."

Startled, she looked up to find him standing on the balcony, watching her. Butterflies fluttered in her chest at the sight of him. "I don't like weeds."

"It shows. Your garden is beautiful. I enjoy it."

Small talk—they'd come back to that. "Thank you. It's not very big and I have a lot more than I can do with it, but with all the work that I'm doing on restoring this place, there's not as much time in the garden as I would like."

"It looks great to me."

She glanced around the small, private space. "The guest garden is really lovely. I actually had landscapers come in and do it because I knew I didn't have time and I needed it to be pretty for my guests. I don't think you've been out there yet. You might enjoy it."

He sat on the edge of the balcony railing and smiled. She ignored the trembling of her stomach looking up at him, thinking about their last meeting in the bathroom. *She wouldn't think about that.*

"No, I haven't been out there. Why do I have to go out there when I can just sit here on this balcony and enjoy your garden? And see you too."

She pulled her gloves off. "Well, you're right, actually, that is one of the pluses for that room. But you know, I don't have any other people coming here for another week. You're very welcome to use any area of the bed-and-breakfast that you'd like for your writing. You don't have to stay holed up there in your room, unless you want to. But if you go back there in the garden, it's really quite beautiful. There's a table, and with the summer breeze and the shade, it's really wonderful. And your hostess, that would be me, would leave you alone. Unless you would like her to bring you an icy glass of lemonade or sweet tea or unsweetened tea. Or water. Not that I'm trying to convince you to get out of that room since I know you were already out today."

He was contemplating her rambling; she could see it in his eyes even from the distance between them.

"The room looks great, by the way. Thanks for changing the sheets and freshening up the bathroom. The flowers were a nice gesture."

Her mouth went dry thinking about him in nothing but a towel and a smile. "Great. Glad you liked it," she said, far too cheerily.

He grinned a bit wickedly. "I'll sleep well tonight in fresh sheets that smell of…lilac, I think."

"Yes. You're right." She didn't want to think about him sleeping in the bed above hers. Well technically he was since there wasn't a bed in the room between them. She was probably not going to sleep again tonight. "How was your outing?"

"Interesting. Not as interesting as finding you in my bathroom, mind you. Not many things will top that. Seriously, are you okay? It's not every day that I nearly scare a woman to death, and I'm afraid that's probably what I did when I came out of that shower. You were completely not expecting me."

"That's an understatement. I was completely not expecting all of that, you know…that you have going on."

He laughed. "And what does that mean?"

Her cheeks heated with a blush. "You know exactly what I mean. My goodness, do you work out at the gym every day?"

"No. I'm in this room, but at my home I have a gym and while I'm on the road, if I can't write or I can't think, I exercise. You know, push-ups, sit-ups, squats. I carry bands with me everywhere I go. Exercise gets your brain to working. It's not all about muscles, although staying fit is important. Why, do my muscles bother you?" He hitched that teasing brow.

"No, of course not," she huffed.

"Are you sure? You seem flustered."

The man was baiting her. "This conversation is really going way off the rails," she said indignantly. "I was asking you if you wanted to use the garden for your writing?"

"And you were implying that me holing up in this room might not be good for me."

"Yes, I was implying that. One of the specifications for when your agent booked this place—and paid me handsomely, I might add—was that I feed you and give you whatever you needed to help stir your creativity. You've altered the food specifications but I realized I hadn't offered you the use of the garden. And it is beautiful." *There, that should get them back on the right footing.*

"Then, I would be happy to come down there and sit in the garden and see if I can write there. But, I'm doing pretty good here. I told you, I wrote all night."

"Yes, you did say that. But, you're very moody. I think it might be good to have balance in your life."

Now he looked at her as though she were a bit

intrusive and a little bit loony.

"Seriously, balance is good."

"Right. I do need balance. I have a proposition."

She dusted her gloves off. "A proposition? Like what?"

"I have an idea for a book. Not the same book that I'm writing right now—a different book. And I need a different perspective. This week, could you show me around this town, like from the perspective of a local? Show me what about it you love. I don't want to see the tourist end of it. You know, if I were to try this book, it would be a different perspective for me. A different book entirely. I need to understand things from the eyes of someone who has lived here. It will give me a new perspective than if I was creating in an intrigue."

She stared at him. "You're writing a romance? You aren't serious?"

"Hold on to your hat. I didn't say I was writing a romance, but I might want to write a different type of book. Not exactly the book we were teasing about last night but—something with a little more heart in it than

I have now? A love interest, maybe? What do you say? Are you game?"

She couldn't believe what she was hearing. "Wow."

Could she spend time with him? The feelings she felt when she was around him were growing and there was no denying it. The man was obviously going to leave at the end of two months, three at the most. He'd go back to his life, he'd finish his book, everything here would go back to normal, and if she was lucky, her B&B would survive. But if she let herself get closer to him…knowing that she was falling for him already, she would be treading on dangerous territory.

She hadn't reacted to a man in quite some time. She hadn't been joking when she told her friends that she thought all of her butterflies had shriveled up and died, or something like that. She hadn't felt truly drawn to a man in such a long time. But she felt an extraordinary connection to Nash and it scared her. There was the very real possibility that she could lose her heart to this man if she weren't careful. Or even if she were careful.

"You did make that agreement with Natalie," he prompted.

He was a wicked man, reminding her of her duty. She took a deep breath and met his gaze. "You're on."

His smile was wide. And every cell in her body told her to run for the hills. But she was mesmerized by him, and stunned because she was not used to seeing such pleasure on his serious face. He was so amazingly handsome and even more handsome like this. And she didn't miss how pleased her decision made him. He looked almost eager. It was completely out of character for him.

Her knees felt weak. "Then I guess we'll start tomorrow. We'll go see whatever you want to see."

"How about if we start right now? It's dinnertime, and I was fairly rude to you last night. Like you said, I was moody. Let me make it up to you. You tell me where the locals go, and we're going to dinner—local style."

She looked down at herself and the dirt on her pants. "That sounds good, but tonight, I'm changing. Give me thirty minutes and I'll meet you in the lobby."

"I'll see you there."

He winked at her—at least, she thought it was a wink. He was so high up there, it was hard to tell. He could have been blinking to get the sun out of his eyes, but then the sun was behind him so that wasn't it. He turned and disappeared back behind the railing and she continued to stare at the sky where he'd been seconds before. The man confused her in ways she couldn't explain. Her hand went to her stomach, where it churned with uncertainty.

What had she gotten herself into?

They went to dinner at a local restaurant that served all types of dishes, not just seafood. There were several locals there, and she introduced him around to people he might not have met. He was no longer incognito, and people had heard he was in town. They were excited to meet him. Erin took advantage of this, thinking maybe the man needed to be around people who wouldn't hound him to death, but would welcome him.

That's what she found so wonderful about Sunset Bay. Everybody was welcoming and friendly. And she had warned him that just like at the festival, people would want to talk to him. And until he became a regular sight around town that would probably be the norm. To her surprise, he didn't seem to mind. In fact, he asked questions of those who stopped to talk to him. What did they like to do? Where were their favorite spots, and why? She found herself observing and enjoying herself. *Where had the uptight man who had arrived here gone?* He truly seemed relaxed. And happy. And she was all the more attracted to him.

She had it bad.

"This is great," he said as they slid into their booth at last.

It hit her suddenly as she looked across the table at him. "You really enjoy creating new settings and characters. Turning over ideas and sorting through them as you create."

He cupped his hands on the table and met her gaze. "I do. You're right. Creating the setting and the new characters that fill the books is my favorite part.

But I have to say that this new idea is something so different than I've ever done. It has me jazzed more than I expected."

"Okay, I'm very curious about this new book. If it's not a romance, then what is it?"

"It's going to be about a family living in a small town, quirky townsfolks, and the family dynamic, with problems and emotions. Honestly, it's not all in focus yet. That's what this exploration is about. I'm getting the feel for it and letting the story come to me."

She was intrigued. "Is that how it is normally done?"

"By me, yes. But every writer has their own way of creating their story. This is my way."

"I find it fascinating."

He cocked his head to the side and his eyes darkened. "Do you find *me* fascinating?"

She straightened in her seat, shocked by his question and not sure she could form an answer without giving away how much she was falling for him.

He reached across the table and took one of her hands in his. "Because I find you fascinating."

Her heart stalled in her chest and her breath caught. *How did she answer him?* Would he run if he knew she had developed feelings for him? He'd run last night.

"You do?" she asked cautiously, very aware that anyone watching them would see him holding her hand.

He arched one dark brow. "I do. Very much so."

Her mouth was dirt dry and she tugged her hand from his and reached for the water the waitress had set on their table. "I need a drink." She gulped the water, and willed her now galloping heart to slow down. She was a grown woman with a good head on her shoulders. She did not need to let herself get carried away with feelings that threatened to overwhelm her. Thankfully, the waitress came and took their order, giving her time to get her head straight.

"You're going to love the pizza. It's wonderful. The best I've ever had."

"Don't be nervous, Erin." He took her hand again.

Was he kidding? How could she not be nervous with him holding her hand like that? "I'm not," she lied and looked about the room. "This diner is nothing special, certainly not on the scale of a national chain. It's a mom-and-pop shop, and Nel and Andre, the owners, have been serving pizza here for about twenty-five to thirty years. I first remember coming here when I was about ten, maybe earlier. When I think about my past, everything melts together. One thing I know about this little joint is that it's always been in my memories." His hand was warm and completely distracting.

"I like it. It's got character. And things that mean something to you. Things that connect locals together for my story. I want readers to feel the ambiance of the environment, and it can't be just cardboard. Even a beach town is more than just beach food and beaches. It's the sum of the people who inhabit it. That's what I'm looking for. This is great."

"Perfect. Then you'll love this next spot," she

said, feeling more comfortable now. And when the pizza came and he had released her hand, she missed it immediately.

She took him to the long pier so he could watch some of the locals who didn't have boats fish from the pier. "I love eating ice cream and watching the tourists and locals reeling in fish from this dock. You can fish, if you'd like. Do you like ice cream?"

"You're talking ice cream—you're talking my language. I don't know about the fishing from a pier but I can do the ice cream."

"My kind of man." She laughed, remembering he didn't like wade fishing but preferred deep sea fishing.

They ordered ice cream and took seats on the bench at the end of the long, wide pier and stared out at the ocean. The waves were rolling in at a rate that brought a cool breeze. Songs that made you know you were at the beach played over the loudspeakers: "Old Blue Chair" by Kenny Chesney, "Toes in the Water" by Zack Brown Band, and several by Jimmy Buffet. New songs mixed with older songs and all with the ability to cause a person to relax. They listened and licked on their ice cream. There was a covered bench at the end of the pier and a couple of pelicans sat on top of it watching for scraps of fish they could sweep in and scoop up.

"Where do you like to fish the most? What location?" she asked, feeling the need to say something. And she was interested in learning more about him than was listed in the magazines or his online biography.

He took a bite of his rocky road ice cream and cocked his head to look at her. "Last time, I took two weeks in the Florida Keys. But I've fished off the coast of Australia when I was there researching a book. I like the Keys, though. I figured that would be where Natalie booked me a room. But I asked her where she heard about your place. She said she saw an ad on her computer when she was searching the rental sites. Your place came across her screen and she felt a pull to it from the photos and decided maybe somewhere new would be good for me. I've holed up in Marathon, near the Seven Mile Bridge a lot. I like it there, but Natalie was right. Change was good for me."

"My cousin Shar Sinclair does a lot of work with the Sea Turtle Rescue Hospital there. She is Shar Lancaster now. I still haven't gotten used to the fact that she's married. Even though Gage is a fabulous man, and I'm thrilled for her, it's hard to get used to because I never pictured Shar as the marrying type."

He paused with his spoon halfway to his mouth. "Why?"

"She's too independent. When we were young, she and I used to say we were not going to get married. We had too many things to do." She smiled. "You have to know my cousin—she was born passionate about things. The moment she saw her first sea turtle and realized the dangers of the waters she loved and they lived in, she became dedicated to saving them. Her parents took the family to Marathon when she was young, I think she was about five, and they visited the sea turtle hospital. She took their card, the one with their rescue number on it, and memorized it. She could repeat the number to anyone who asked about it. And that fixation continued on into adult life."

"That's interesting. I was like that about writing stories. But what about you? You said you were passionate about something but didn't say what it was."

"Actually, I said that because we were together and I let her love of it wear off on me while I was around her. When we came home, I got busy in my regular life and wasn't as passionate. When I saw a sea turtle in trouble, I knew who to call and I did and still do. But Shar, she's different. She goes out every morning in search of sea turtles stranded on the beach or sick or injured in the water. There is a huge difference. I guess my real passion didn't show up until I opened my B&B. I'm passionate about making it the best for my guests. I just need more guests."

"You'll have them." He studied her. "Your cousin sounds like the few of us born knowing what we were meant to do and be. I think most people are like you—they discover it as they age, if they are lucky. I know some people never discover it, or never let themselves dream enough to discover it. And your place will be a success."

She bit the chocolate ice cream from her spoon, letting his words sink in as the flavors burst through her with goodness. "True. I had several hobbies growing up but nothing that stuck except I loved helping my mother when she prepared for parties. She's a wonderful host. Shar's mother is too."

His brows dipped. "You are too. A little pushy sometimes." He laughed and she pushed his arm.

"Okay, wise guy."

"Only because you wanted to make my stay great."

"True," she said. They stared at each other for a long moment and her stomach dipped. It was such a dangerous feeling, knowing that there was something about this man that drew her to him in unexplained and undeniable ways. She could lean forward and place a kiss on his lips if she were brave enough. If she dared. But she had never been a daredevil. She smiled, instead. "Whether you wanted me to or not," she said, in a breathy voice she didn't recognize. And despite the fact that she was a coward, she swayed toward him.

"Exactly," he murmured, looking every bit as ready to kiss her as she was to kiss him.

"You two look cozy."

Hearing Jonah's voice, Erin sprang back from Nash and looked guiltily at her brother, who stood next to the railing of the pier. He held an ice cream cone of his own and smiled knowingly from her to Nash.

"Jonah." Her heart pounded so hard from the near kiss—then add in his surprising her and she felt as if her head were going to explode from all the blood being pumped into it.

"Oh, don't stop on my account." He grinned. "I was enjoying people watching after a long day on the boat and when I realized my sister was part of the couple getting cozy over here. I decided it would be rude for me to walk by and ignore you."

Erin was not buying his story. He was messing with her and now all the family would probably hear that she and Nash had been cozy on the pier.

Nash chuckled gruffly. "Jonah, you have terrible timing. But you already know that."

"Yeah, couldn't help myself. I've been told before." He grinned and took a lick of his chocolate ice cream. "You two didn't come by and take a boat ride the other day. What happened?"

"My fault. I got to working and the words were flowing. I tend to lose track of time when that happens."

Not exactly what had happened, but it was close enough.

"The offer stands. Come by any time. Okay, I'm heading home. I just stopped by here after work. It was a hot one out on the water today."

They both told him goodnight and then Nash stood and held out his hand to her. "Ready to head back home?"

The sound of him calling the B&B home hit her

and she liked the sound of it far too much. But as she slipped her hand into Nash's and felt the firm, tantalizing feel of it closing around hers, she knew as she stood and walked slowly beside him down the boardwalk that everything about them felt right.

Except for the fact that he was leaving.

CHAPTER TWELVE

When they arrived back at the B&B, the sun was setting. Nash waited beside her as she unlocked the door. The tension between them was thick and she knew he felt it too because his hand on hers had grown tighter as they got nearer to the B&B.

She had never been with anyone she had felt so comfortable with, and yet, so tense. It was strange because when he had first arrived, she would have never, ever envisioned that she could be comfortable with him at all, and yet, sitting on the pier with him, it felt as if they'd been watching sunsets together for a lifetime. Now, though, comfortable wasn't the word that fit what was happening between them. She was tense, frustrated, a ball of nerves and anticipation... *Was he going to kiss her now?*

She told herself not to think such things, he was her guest. And that just seemed wrong.

She quickly unlocked the door and then hurried down the back entrance and into the kitchen. Needing something to do, she walked to the coffee pot. "I think I'll make some fresh coffee. Can I get you anything?"

There—she was the hostess again. She wasn't this strange hopeful, wishful person she had become somewhere between dinner at the pizza bar, the dock, and now here. Her fingers fumbled as she tried to separate a liner for the filter. He didn't answer her; she glanced over her shoulder and saw him next to the island in the center of the room, watching her. Her breath caught in her throat and she fought not to throw herself at the man. Instead, she spun back to the counter and fumbled with the coffee canister lid, her fingers trembled. The lid finally popped open, flew across the counter and dropped to the floor. The loud noise sounded like an alarm in the room. She closed her eyes and tried to calm down.

"Erin." He'd moved behind her. "Look at me."

Her heart pounded so hard she felt dizzy. *She would not look at him; she would not.* Instead, she swallowed the lump in her throat and willed her nerves and the freaking butterflies to calm down. To her surprise, he moved even closer and she could feel the heat from his body almost touching hers. He reached around her and took the coffee filter from her hands. He set it on the counter then turned her to face him.

"I get that I'm your guest in this house, and I don't mean to make you uncomfortable. But Erin, I really enjoyed myself this evening. I've enjoyed myself every time I'm near you. I can sense that that makes you uncomfortable."

She could barely hear his words for her hammering heart. It took all of the willpower she possessed to stand where she was standing and not to lean forward into his space. "It's just that I'm not used to this. I'm your host. To tell the truth, I never even thought about...okay, we're both grown-ups here. I never thought about what would happen if I had a guest and I was attracted to him." There, she had said it. Loud and clear. His lip twitched and his dark eyes glittered mischievously. Or, she should say wickedly. He was enjoying her uncomfortable circumstances. "You are not helping this situation at all."

His lips twitched. "No, I'm not." He tugged her into his arms, and she went easily, leaning against him with her cheek resting on his hard chest. It was heaven. She couldn't move, just savored the feel of him holding her.

"Erin, this is where I've wanted you to be all evening. I can't stop thinking about you. But I also understand the position that you're in." He leaned back and with one hand, cupped her chin and tilted her head back so he could look into her eyes. "I had to hold you for a moment."

He had wanted her in his arms all evening?

It was almost too unbelievable to think about. And while she was thinking about it, he dipped his head and kissed her.

The moment his firm lips covered hers, the room

began to spin. Her world as she had known it tilted and slid right off the edge of a cliff and into another dimension. She had never, ever felt anything like this before. She reveled in the feel of his lips against hers. Of his strong arms tightening around her. Of her own hands plastered against his chest, gripping his shoulders as she clung to him, and to her joy the kiss went on and on. And it could have kept going as far as she was concerned—she was incapable of coherent thought. Oh, she knew that tomorrow she would be very regretful. But right now, in this moment, she was not.

Not at all.

Nash kissed Erin as though he were a starving man. And he was. His brain was scattered and all over the place. The only thought that he had was that kissing Erin was the best thing he had ever done in his life. Holding her, feeling her arms around him felt like home and that was something that Nash craved. She was nice, and kind and beautiful and made him feel and want things he'd never had or known before.

His father had made him a home, but even that home didn't feel like what it felt like to be in Erin's arms, in Erin's kitchen, in Erin's world.

He deepened the kiss as emotions flooded him. His arms tightened and she felt like heaven in his embrace when she melted against him. Nash fought for sanity and after what seemed like an endless, breathtaking, ongoing moment he forced himself to break the kiss.

She looked as shaken as he felt. They stared at each other. The power of what had just happened between them, of the connection that had gone out of control, had them both stunned. She backed away from him looking unsteady as she leaned against the counter.

Grasping the edge as she looked at him. "That was some kiss," she whispered, sounding as if her voice hadn't come back to her yet. She lifted her fingertips and touched her lips.

"Yes, some kiss," he managed, wanting to pull her back into his arms. She was so beautiful, so good...and he knew he didn't have what it took to take a relationship to a deeper level. What was he doing?

She tilted her head. "For a writer, you are not always a man of words."

He gave her an apologetic look. "I tend to go inside myself when I'm feeling emotions I'm not used to feeling."

Her eyes widened and grew soft as she realized he'd just said she'd brought out emotions he wasn't used to feeling. She was so lovely, with her flushed skin and sparkling eyes that studied him as if she too were feeling new emotions. His heart clenched, and ached with the realization that he was not good for her. He couldn't—

"I know how you feel." A hint of a smile curved her lips, drawing his gaze and sending his pulse thundering once more.

He needed to get his head clear. "I better head to my room. I hope I didn't mess anything up between us."

She shook her head slightly. "You didn't." Her voice was weak. She wasn't saying much herself.

He pushed away from the counter. But instead of heading toward the stairs he leaned forward and gently kissed her on her cheek. "Goodnight, Erin."

And then he headed through the house and up three flights of stairs to his room and firmly closed the door between them.

All he could think about was Erin in his arms.

CHAPTER THIRTEEN

The next morning, Erin had a meeting with Rosie and Lulu about Lulu and Brad's wedding. They had finally agreed to a date and she had to say, she was happy that they had not chosen to fly to Las Vegas in secret like Adam and Rosie had done. For one, she was happy about this because her poor mother—though thrilled that Adam and Rosie were married, because the sooner they got married the sooner she would have a grandchild—still she would have liked to have been at the first wedding of her children. Erin had told Brad that she hoped he would give their mother, the opportunity to see him and Lulu get married.

Of course, when she'd told Brad that, he didn't reveal to her that that he and Lulu had picked a date already. *The sneak!* That was just like Brad, keeping things to himself just to tease her and torture her.

When Lulu called the meeting to discuss the date, she had been thrilled. She loved Lulu. She had just gotten to know Lulu over the past few months, but she was perfect for Brad. Both of her brothers had done very well in their choices even though four or five months ago, she had never dreamed that either of them would be ready to settle down. And yet, here they were, one married and the other soon to be. She couldn't wait to hear what the date was, and she was so happy to have an excuse to leave the B&B and get away from Nash. All she could think about all morning and night was his kiss…

She sighed wistfully. That kiss had been mind-boggling. She'd felt…so much. An overload of emotions.

There was no denying that she wanted more of it. *More, more, more!* Every molecule of her being sang out with force.

She had fallen fast and hard.

It was the truth.

And it scared her to death.

She wanted Nash Bond.

She wanted everything about him.

Everything that had to do with him…she just wanted *him*.

How could an attraction like that happen so quickly? Of course, that was a stupid question. Attraction always happened quickly. But this was far more than simple attraction, her heart was involved.

This was a force that could not stop, could not be understood…but could it be denied?

Brad and Lulu had fallen quickly too and Rosie and Adam had fallen in love lightning fast—at least, in her world it was lightning fast—and neither couple had wanted to deny or stop their love, at least not that she knew of.

But she was not the type to risk letting herself fall into love so easily. No, ever since she'd realized last night that she was indeed falling in love with Nash, she'd felt as if she was free falling without a safety net.

She stepped onto the sidewalk then paused to rub her blurry, gritty eyes. She knew she looked like heck.

She was in terrible trouble too. He wasn't the kind of man who would settle in a small town like this, and she wasn't moving. And the man probably kissed a woman like he'd kissed her, at every chance he got.

She needed coffee and a muffin. Two muffins. Shoot, she needed a muffin, a cinnamon roll, and maybe a buttercream cupcake. And another cup of coffee.

Strong, black, cappuccino, espresso.

She needed all of it. She was in so much trouble.

The moment she entered the door of Bake My Day, she had Rosie and Lulu's attention. And Gigi's too. She was at the coffeemaker, and the blonde's eyes widened as she looked at Erin. "Girl, you need a coffee. Coming right up."

Rosie, who was sitting at the counter going through receipts, dropped her pen, shot to her feet and rushed from behind the counter. "Erin, you look terrible. What's happened?"

Lulu, who must have been sitting at a table and Erin hadn't noticed, hurried over, coffee in hand. "*What* has happened to *you*? Drink this, you need it more than I do." She shoved her coffee cup into Erin's hand. She took a long swig.

"Yes, what happened?" Rosie took her arm. "You look like you didn't sleep for days. You barely even brushed your hair. Has something happened?"

She hadn't brushed her hair! She smoothed her hair with her hands. *How could she have forgotten to brush her hair?* She brushed her teeth; she washed her face. Sure, she put on clothes. But she hadn't brushed her hair. *How could this have happened?*

She groaned. "I've fallen in love." She sank into the chair, propped her elbow on the table, and dropped her forehead to her palm. "I'm so confused."

Lulu and Rosie took seats on either side of her.

"Did you say you fell in love?" Lulu asked.

"That's what I heard," Rosie said.

"It's true." Erin looked at both of them. "He's going to leave. He hasn't been here for a month yet and I'm helplessly in love with the man. How could I have let this happen?"

Gigi placed a big yellow ceramic cup in front of her. It was full of black brew. "I made it extra strong because I can tell when a woman needs an extra strong cup of coffee. Drink up and then take it from the top." Gigi looked concerned. "Rosie, maybe you and Lulu need to take her somewhere quieter. I can handle the rush when it comes in but maybe she doesn't need a lot of people seeing her this way."

"You're right." Rosie stood. "Lulu, let's go to your place."

"Good idea." Lulu stood up too grabbed her paper cup of coffee and handed Gigi the big yellow mug. "Pour this in a to-go cup, Gigi, and we'll hightail it out of here."

Rosie nodded. "The last thing we need is Lila or Mami coming in here. Or even Birdie or Doreen."

"Gotcha."

Erin watched in a daze, suddenly wondering why she'd even come here to confess her gargantuan mess-up. Nothing could change what she'd done.

Within moments, she was being ushered down the

quiet street to Lulu's Pet Paradise doggy daycare and B&B for man's best friends. She should have started a dog B&B, pets were less complicated.

They didn't go into the business, where Lulu's staff was watching over the half a dozen dogs that had already been delivered that morning, or picked up by them. Instead, Lulu led the way up the stairs to her apartment on the second floor of the building. By the time they'd walked inside the cute three-room apartment, Erin had had several drinks of the strong coffee and felt a little more clearheaded and not quite as desperate. Okay, she was desperate, she just had gotten her emotions pulled back and felt a little more in control.

Once they all sat down around the small table in Lulu's kitchen area, Rosie patted her arm. "Now, tell us. What in the world is going on."

Lulu pushed the coffee cup toward her. "Take another sip of this and then tell us about you and Nash."

Instead of looking upset, Lulu looked absolutely delighted.

Erin frowned. "Why don't you look shocked? You look excited. Happy."

Lulu had the decency to blush. "I've been hoping for this. I like him, and he has the seal of approval from Lila, Mami, Birdie, and Doreen. That's like a gold crown. It's a stamp of excellence. Tell her, Rosie!"

Rosie looked sympathetic. "I'm so sorry you look very unhappy, but it's true. We've all been hoping he might sweep you off your sensible feet."

"Sensible feet?" She stared at Rosie.

"You have them firmly locked on a path you don't deviate from at all. So yes, sensible feet. I was hoping he might put some excitement in to your life. And some romance."

"She's right," Lulu gushed. "Nash was in the bakery the other day when I was there with Lila and the girls and he had us all rolling. He was just a delight. He talked about stories he had written and things he had seen, and he won me over and all of us. We were hoping there might be something between you two."

Rosie's eyes softened. "I like him a lot, and I told Adam that you and him would make a wonderful couple. Adam took my word for it, and he's in hopes that maybe something could come of it for you."

"You've been talking to my brothers about me and Nash?"

Lulu held up her hand as if she were swearing on a Bible. "I'm guilty too. I told Brad. And you know Brad—he was teasing and saying that maybe you two might beat us to the altar, but I told him that wasn't going to happen. So, that's when we set our date."

"Seriously? You set your wedding date so that you might beat me and Nash Bond to the altar?" the words came out almost hysterically. *"Have you lost your mind?"*

"Funny. But it was a good excuse to go ahead and do the deed. I'm ready. I don't want to wait any longer. Brad wanted to stretch it out a little bit because he was worried about me, you know? Worried that I had been through so much and that he shouldn't rush me. I'm ready to be rushed. I'm not like his ex, and he's not like my ex. We're not going to stand each other up at the altar, therefore we might as well get this thing done so we can get on to happily-ever-after. And you know, I've got my business started and I've got all my puppies down there and it's going great. I'm over the moon happy. And, to tell you the truth, I'm ready for a baby, and I know your mama is ready for a baby. And I don't know about Rosie and Adam, if they're planning on having one any time soon, but honestly, I wouldn't mind if I had a baby tomorrow. I haven't broken that news to your brother yet but I will."

This news brought Erin from her stupor. "Wow."

Rosie laughed. "Lulu! When you move, you move fast."

Lulu giggled. "I'm in love and I feel like I was unhappy for so long, and now I'm so happy I could burst. Here, you drink that coffee, Erin. Because you do look bad. And if you're going to tell us all about how you and Nash fell in love, then drink up and spill. Not spill the coffee, but spill the beans on what's going on. And for crying out loud, don't look like the world is coming to an end, because it's not. You are *in love*. It's a very magical thing."

Erin picked up the coffee cup and took a sip, then calmly took another sip, and then a third sip. While she was taking the sips, she contemplated how to go about this. Her friends and her brothers obviously were in cahoots to marry her off. But Nash was leaving. He was not the kind of man who hung around and lived in one place for forever.

She set her paper coffee cup down. "Okay, girls, he kissed me last night. He kissed me, and it was like nothing I have ever, ever felt before. I think it was partly because, since he's been in the house these short few weeks…I haven't counted all the days, but you know, it hasn't been that long…I just can't stop thinking about him. He was maddening at first. I couldn't really stand him. But then I got to know him and when he kissed me, even before that I knew that I had fallen in love with him."

"I knew you two were a match." Rosie sighed.

"Don't get excited, because he won't ever settle here. This is not a place that a man like him would settle. And remember, he's a guy who does exciting things and I'm about as exciting as a turtle in the road.

I mean, I cross the road as quick as I can to be safe, and he's dropping out of airplanes? Seriously, girls, we are not a match. And yet, when he kissed me, I felt like I had been longing for his love all my life and my world was now complete."

Rosie and Erin stared at each other, and Rosie's smile grew on her face.

She looked at Lulu, she smiled, her bright-red hair shining in the fluorescent light and her eyes glittering with happiness. "I think it's just marvelous. And you know what I decided?" Lulu looked from Rosie to Erin. They both shook their heads. "I decided that sometimes, things just don't make sense. And that's okay. Because the heart knows what's what, and it makes sense out of nonsense sometimes. So, go give it a chance, Erin. Your heart has it figured out—you just have to get that cautious mind of yours to get on board."

Erin let Lulu's words roll around in her brain for a minute, not exactly sure she got the exact meaning of what Lulu was saying. "And you used to be a lawyer?"

Lulu nodded. "I was. But of course, I didn't do

prosecutions or anything like that, because sometimes I ramble and that wouldn't have been too good. But, that's my closing statement. Sometimes life just doesn't make sense, but if you want to be happy, sometimes you have to grab it by the horns and go with it."

"She is right," Rosie said. "I almost died and I'm saying take a chance. Have you and him talked? Has he told you he wouldn't want to stay here? Because I can tell you, he's looked quite comfortable here every time I've seen him."

She sighed. "No, I haven't actually talked to him about that. We hadn't even gotten that far. We…we're really just starting to get to know each other. There's such a pull between us that we couldn't really deny the kiss last night. And then we both ran into our rooms and locked the doors. I think we were afraid of each other, or afraid of ourselves. I was really glad when you told me you wanted me to come over here this morning so I could get away from him. Let me get another sip of coffee and then we're going to quit talking about me and you can tell me and Rosie what date you and my brother are getting married." She took a long sip of the hot brew and let it burn all the way from her throat into her belly. She hoped those butterflies got their wings singed, because they sure had been giving her fits lately.

She calmed down a little bit. Life would come back into perspective, and she would get a grip, and things would go back to normal. After all, she was a sensible girl. "Now, when are you and Brad getting married?"

Lulu laughed. "We're getting married in three weeks. Do you think we can pull a wedding together in three weeks?"

"Three weeks?" Rosie gasped. "Are you kidding? With the group that we have that'll be coming and getting this done, sure we can. It'll be beautiful. I tell you what, Mami Desmond can pull a wedding together so fast. Or, if you want a real wedding planner, who is supposed to be opening up down the street. I'm sure she'll be looking for business."

"Nope, I don't want a wedding planner. I think we can all do it. You know me—I'm real plain, and I think all of us together can create something simple but beautiful. And in the end, I come out of it a married woman to the most wonderful man in all the world."

Erin stared at Lulu. She was completely overwhelmed, baffled, and intrigued. But that was the truth: a wedding was about the person you were marrying, and everything else was icing on the cake. It didn't have to be a big deal. The big deal was that you were marrying the man of your dreams.

Instantly, Erin thought of Nash Bond. Never, ever in her wildest dreams would she have thought of Nash Bond as her dream man. Talk about dreaming big. She would have never even thought to think about the man. But now he'd stormed into her world and he was all she could imagine. All she could dream of or hope for.

She was doomed.

CHAPTER FOURTEEN

Nash shut his computer and rubbed the bridge of his nose with his fingers. It was no use; he wanted, needed to talk to Erin. Since kissing her the night before he'd stayed holed up in his room hiding.

He hadn't written any words, no, he'd just stared at the computer screen and replayed how right Erin had felt in his arms. When they'd kissed. When they'd spent time together.

He'd enjoyed every moment when he was with her. The kiss had rocked his world and made him want more than he'd ever let himself think about.

He wasn't the settling down kind of man. He was a loner. Always had been, and yet, he wanted desperately to ask her again to show him more of Sunset Bay through her eyes, something he had enjoyed. But after the kiss, he'd known more time with her would only tempt him to kiss her again. And what good would that do? He was leaving. He always left.

His past had haunted him all day. Taunted him. Told him he wasn't good enough to stay. He'd stayed in his room and worked—no, he'd stared at his computer screen. He was a grown man of thirty-five, and yet, he sometimes felt like the lost boy he'd been before his dad, Gerald, had rescued him. He stood and paced the room, the walls caving in around him.

He didn't have what it took to be in a relationship. Erin probably had already figured out that he wasn't a man who could be counted on.

He'd said he was taking her boating and hadn't. He'd said he wanted her to show him around and after one evening, he'd called it off and run to his room where he buried himself in his work or tried to... Like always he'd tried to hide inside the words of the world he was creating. But he'd never felt the way he felt right now. It had never felt wrong until now.

He headed downstairs. Erin was in the kitchen right where they had been standing the night before when he'd kissed her. She was mixing something in a bowl and had her back to him. Her blonde hair hung loose and she wore jean shorts that came mid-thigh and a plain T-shirt of some kind of soft material that shimmered every time she stirred the contents of the bowl. Her outfit was conservative and plain, and yet, he'd never wanted to slip his arms around a woman and pull her close more than he wanted Erin.

He still had time to turn away and go back up to his room and throw himself into the book. He was leaving. He didn't need to get involved. He had been through that already, and yet, the desire to spend time with Erin overpowered everything.

"Erin, do you have anything planned for today?"

She spun, hand on her heart. "You scared me."

"I'm sorry." He held his hands out, wanting to touch her, to ease her surprise but he stayed where he was and gave her a chance to adjust. He watched her surprise fade and a mixture of hurt and wariness took over.

She didn't trust him and the knowledge stung. "Do you have any plans?" he asked again, more determined now than ever to get her to agree to go out with him.

She looked confused. "I'm getting your supper ready. And then I'm going to go back out to the garage and work on a table I'm staining for one of the guest rooms. Is there something I can get you?"

So impersonal. That was his fault. She knew better than anyone that he was leaving. His reservation had an end date, it was written in her guest book. To make it more official, he'd kissed her last night and then pulled away again. What was she supposed to think? He had dropped the ball in so many instances.

"Nothing you can get me, but you can come with me. I called your brother and he has a boat waiting for us. It's about time I took you on that boat ride I've kept bailing on you about. How about a sunset boat ride?"

The wariness intensified. "It's late."

"We have about six hours before dark if you think about it. And it will end with a beautiful sunset. Could you show me around in that amount of time?"

She didn't react, simply stood very still. And the look in her eyes did not bode well. But he kept his mouth closed and waited. He'd put the ball in her court and hoped she'd say yes. He was a grown man, and yet, he felt like he was an eighth grader asking his first girl crush to the school dance. He hadn't ever gone to a school dance. He hadn't even been attending school until Gerald had taken him off the street and given him a home—he pushed the thoughts out of his brain. And focused on the beautiful woman in front of him he wanted her to say yes.

"Are you sure about this? After last night, I thought maybe we needed to get this, whatever is between us, back on track with you as my guest and me as your hostess."

"That might be the smartest thing," he said, keeping his voice steady. "And if that's what you want then that's what we will do. I have another month on the books here. Another month to work on the book so to speak and I could go back up there and stay in that room pounding those keys. That would be the smart thing for me to do but, Erin, I didn't get a word written today. All I thought about was you. No matter what I tell myself or how hard I try, the only thing I want right now is for you to go on a boat ride with me. What do you say? What do you want?"

Emotion flickered in her eyes it warmed him and his chest tightened as he waited for her to speak.

She took a deep breath and tension eased. "I want to go on a boat ride and see the coastline of Sunset Bay with you."

Yes. Relief washed through him and he couldn't even smile, he felt as if he'd just changed the balance of his life. He crossed into the room and held his hand out to her and as if it was just as big a step for her she studied his hand, her gaze flickered to his before she placed her hand in his.

Jonah was standing beside the boat when they arrived. Her brother had a grin on his face as they walked up. Jonah so good-natured, such a catch if some female in Sunset Bay could come along and win his heart. To her, he was her brother and he seemed like the most uncomplicated person she knew. He loved Sunset Bay, he loved his business and he loved life. And he, as far as she knew, wanted to settle down with a wife and family one day. He might not come out and say that, but his manner and actions spoke those words loud and clear to anybody observant enough to look at it. The man beside her on the other hand was complicated, a rover full of wanderlust and a man who was moody and buried himself in the books he wrote. As far as his life spoke if you looked at it was that he didn't want a wife, he didn't want to settle down and he didn't want anything that could complicate his life.

And yet, he had asked her to go on this boat ride and they both knew that in him doing that he had swung open the door to complicate his life.

She'd stepped through that door willingly knowing full well that he still might leave. What if he left? She had already fallen for him, she had admitted it that morning when she was with Rosie and Lulu. And in the hour since their talk in Lulu's apartment and all that strong coffee that she had drank to clear her head, Erin knew that for her, there was no going back because she had fallen in love with Nash Bond the man she'd come to know and wanted to know more.

Some might say it didn't speak well for her intelligence. And she might agree and when he left her tiny town and never looked back. She might even one day tell herself that this was the stupidest move she had ever made in her entire life. But right now, she didn't care because she was taking a risk.

When he had come down those stairs and asked her to go on this boat ride with him, she'd hoped he was on the verge of opening up a little bit of his heart to her. He created worlds in the books he wrote that had big adventures for his readers and satisfying endings. But his own world, his personal world inside that heart of his was very guarded and small.

Nash didn't let anybody into his personal world. And yet, here she stood.

Motoring along the coastline a few minutes later Nash

thought it was gorgeous. He had seen some of the most beautiful coastlines in the world. And yet, there was a calmness to this small stretch of Florida coast that was different to him…the water seemed clearer and sparkled topaz like most of the southern Gulf Coast of Florida but there was peace here, a peace that he'd never found anywhere. Spying two dolphins swimming beside them he pulled back on the boat's throttle, bringing it to a stop to watch them as they flew from the water showing off for him and Erin. They were far enough out from shore that they'd have a view of the sun setting and the lights glowing from the shore. And the dolphins playing. It was perfect.

He glanced over at Erin and knew she was the source of the peace he felt here. Being with Erin felt right.

"Are you enjoying it? Are you glad you came?"

She pushed her beautiful blonde hair back from her face and removed her sunshades. Her eyes sparkled like the ocean around them. "I am very glad I came. I love the coastline. I might not be the most adventurous, most spirited person, but I love getting in a boat and riding around. It's a lovely coastline. But I'm sure that for you, you've seen so much more during your travels and on your writing retreats."

"About that…Erin, I brought you out here so that I could say something. You being here with me makes this the most amazing place I've ever been to." He watched her expression falter. He had never been in a position where he could hurt someone's heart. Or his own. He had never stayed in a relationship long enough to get to this point. And with Erin, he didn't even have a relationship, they'd barely known each other for a month. And yet, they had one.

He took her hands and pulled her from the chair so that she came into his arms. The boat rocked gently beneath them, the smooth as glass blue water surrounded them. He felt her heart thumping against his, hard and fast. He placed a kiss on top of her head, then rested his cheek against her hair and breathed in the sweet scent of her. When she was in his arms contentment settled over him. He had never felt this before.

"I know that you can look at my past and see that I

don't stick around. I've never made any claims that I do. I don't want to hurt you but I can't stop thinking about you." He moved his head so he could look at her and she looked up at him. He wasn't sure what he was asking.

She placed a hand on his heart and her touch was like a lightning strike. He sought the words to say to her, and was afraid he wouldn't find the right ones.

"I know that something in here," she patted his heart with her hand, "struggles. I fear knowing what you might have gone through before your adoptive father found you and rescued you from the life you were living. Though you didn't actually say it, I feel you were hurt deeply in your past as a child. Because of that you've spent your life running and closing people out."

His heart was racing. "Yes," he said, curt and dry. His thoughts reeling from how she read him so clearly.

"You were trying to protect this heart that you've enclosed in steel and determined never to show. Or let anyone inside. Nash, I know I run the risk of you walking out that door when your reservation is up. I've realized I can handle that if it comes to that, if you realize this isn't what is right for you. But what I can't handle is us not exploring what we think we have here."

His arms tightened around her.

"I would like to share these boat rides like this with you. I want to sit on the pier eating ice cream like we did the other night. I want to explore this, I want to give that a try. So, while you're here, when you're not writing, I hope that you'll keep your guard down and let me in here." She tapped his heart again.

His longing for what she was saying nearly split his head open it was pounding so hard through him. "My past, it's…always…" He halted, and started over. "It's as if you looked in my brain and read what I'm thinking, what I'm feeling. How is that?"

For the first time since he had taken her in his arms she looked uncertain. "I think something in your heart speaks to my heart. I think that we are very much alike in aspects of our hearts and very much opposite in aspects of our adventurous spirits. But I think we balance each other out."

Could it be? *Was she falling in love with him like*—he didn't want to admit that he was falling in love with Erin yet. Love changed everything.

Love had the power to hurt so deeply it scarred you for life.

The boat rocked from the wake of another boat passing by. He braced his feet and let his body take the shifting of the boat as his arms tightened around her. She didn't wobble, obviously used to the feel of a boat beneath her feet. She smiled and longing to kiss her, he did.

Her hands moved around his neck and she clung to him, kissing him back. Too soon she pulled away "Don't run away from me again," she said softly, reading him like a book.

"I won't."

CHAPTER FIFTEEN

The next two weeks were spent in a flurry of excitement as they worked diligently on getting ready for Brad and Lulu's wedding. Lulu was floating on cloud nine, scatterbrained and joyful. She was adorable Erin thought and really had her own heart longing to let loose and feel what she was so afraid of admitting to herself, much less anyone else.

"I tell you what, those two can make even a hard case like me grin they are so happy," Birdie said, sitting at the window seat at Bake My Day as the group watched Lulu standing in Brad's arms out on the sidewalk. She was a lot shorter than Erin's brother and they were really cute together. Lulu with her bright red hair, brighter now that the sun had lightened it, and Brad with his dark hair as he bent his head down to look at her, causing Lulu to giggle, something she did a lot of when the fire chief of Sunset Bay was around. And Brad walked around with a grin on his face everywhere he went.

"You are not a hard case," Lila harrumphed. "You have a romantic heart inside that skinny little body of yours. You've just got no filter and don't always say the sappy things you are feeling."

Birdy scowled. "I don't feel sappy things."

"Oh yes you do. But this isn't about you right now, everyone in Sunset Bay is happy for them. They are adorable together. And I'm so glad she's not hiding from him behind corndog stands and shrubs anymore."

"Me too," Doreen said. "I've done my share of hiding from people through my life and it just sucks."

"*Doreen,*" Mami gasped.

Doreen blushed fuchsia as everyone stared at her in dismay. "I'm sorry, I shouldn't have said sucked."

"*No*," they all echoed.

Mami laid a hand on her friend's arm. "I meant, I didn't know you had ever hidden from people. Anyone in particular?"

"That's what I meant too," Lila said and Birdie nodded.

Rosie looked as sad as Erin felt. "Doreen, I know you're shy but I never knew you were that shy."

"I didn't either," Erin agreed feeling terrible for Doreen.

"I got over it mostly, but it was worse when I was longing to date and had a crush on…well someone."

"Who?" Birdie snapped as everyone passed looks of shock amongst themselves while Doreen fiddled with the lace at the bottom of her sleeve.

Who had Doreen had a crush on that caused her to hide, much like Lulu had done from Brad?

"No one. He moved away a long time ago so it's not important. I was just saying that I'm glad Lulu got her man and came out of hiding with her love."

Erin was not going to be able to not be curious about who Doreen's mystery man was. From the looks on Birdie's, Lila's and Mami's faces they weren't either. Doreen had just opened herself up to constant nagging from her friends. Erin would never do that.

She realized that in some ways she was hiding out from what she felt for Nash. She loved him but would she admit that to anyone? No. Especially to him. They had been spending dinners and sometimes lunches together and he'd opened up more and more about how neglected he'd been and the abuse he'd taken as a child, and she'd been honored to know that he trusted her enough to talk to her. But love, she wasn't sure Nash could ever love anyone. She wasn't sure he'd ever let himself love anyone. The betrayal of his parents went too deep. But sitting there in Bake My Day she knew that for her there was no going back.

"Okay, ladies," Rosie said, patting Doreen's hand. "Let's get back to Lulu and Brad's wedding and give Doreen a break. Lila, you're picking up the tableclothes, right?"

"Right."

Erin listened to Rosie go down the checklist so they could all know they had everything handled from the tablecloths to the punch and cookies to the cake and photographer.

They'd all worked really hard on the wedding. It was going to be on the beach. And they had invited friends and family but they had kept it smaller. Some of the family from Windswept Bay was coming not everybody was getting to come but she knew a few of them were and she was excited to see them. As the planning went on, Erin's mind wandered to Nash—it did most every moment these days.

She and Nash had fallen into a routine during the last two weeks. It was comfortable and exciting and she spent her days working with her bed and breakfast, continuing to spruce it up and book guests. Miraculously yesterday the phone had started ringing and people were booking rooms and many were requesting the upper floor room. Wondering what had happened, this morning she'd gone to investigate the review sites. And that was when she saw there was a new review up on a major review site—*Nash had given her a review.*

Not just a review but an unbelievably fantastic

review telling where he wrote and what was so amazing about his favorite writing retreat space.

She'd stopped breathing as she stared at the review. Gratefulness filled her like floodwaters into an empty valley.

As she entered the house, she left behind all thoughts other than finding Nash and thanking him.

He was in the kitchen pouring himself a cup of coffee.

"You wrote a review."

He turned and looked innocent. "Me? Now why would I do that?"

She laughed. "I'm not sure. I hope it's because you have a thing for the B&B owner and also like her B&B." She walked toward him and he set the coffee pot and the mug down and reached for her, drawing her into his arms sending her system flying.

"I have a thing for the B&B owner, it's true. And her B&B is amazing. I hope it helps."

She cupped his face with one hand. "It has already. I have the weekend after the wedding all booked. I could have booked it the weekend of the wedding but my cousins are coming to stay for that weekend."

He smiled. "I'm glad I still have a room booked or you might have rented it out from under me."

"Not a chance."

He kissed her gently. "Good, because I'm going to have a hard time giving my room up before that weekend."

She inhaled slowly trying not to panic, knowing full well that the weekend after the wedding was his last.

"And just to make sure the reviews keep on giving I talked about my room in that interview I did with *People Magazine.*"

"What?" she asked breathless.

"If I knew it would get this reaction I'd have done the interview sooner. I should have done it sooner."

"No, you didn't have to do it at all. But, Nash, I'm so grateful."

"Everything I said was true. And I built the interview around Sunset Bay, the B&B and the writers retreat/honeymoon suite on the third floor. There is a near impossibility that the reporter could edit out references to the bed and breakfast. The interview was contingent on them including info about The Inn at Sunset Bay.'

She couldn't believe it. The phones were already ringing just from the review. She couldn't fathom what exposure in such a huge magazine would do for her business and it would be good for Sunset Bay as well. Everything she had wanted when his agent had first called and booked the room for him was coming true.

So why didn't she feel more excited? Of course, she knew why and she was telling herself to be brave because as far as she knew he was leaving exactly as planned from the beginning.

The wedding was on the beach and it was beautiful. Nash had sat at the back of the seating and watched as Erin and Rosie along with her sister, Cassie, stood beside Lulu on the beach as she married Brad. He had all of his brothers, Adam as best man, Tate and Jonah as groomsmen beside him. Nash watched, unable to take his eyes off of Erin, wanting what he'd never thought he'd want.

The bed and breakfast was full with her female cousins who ran the Windswept Bay Resort and their husbands. Cali and Grant, Shar and Gage, Jillian and Ryan and then Olivia and B.J. Her cousins were great and their husbands were an interesting group. He'd found his mind starting to click as he'd heard how each of the couples had met. Grant was a world-famous sea life artist; Gage was a billionaire businessman. He was still tossing around the idea of setting a series in the small town. He hadn't figured out everything but his mind was still spinning, searching for the pieces that would fit together and lead him to the story he knew was brewing. And yet, as he sat there and watched Erin watching her brother marry the love of his life, Nash wasn't sure once he left if he would be able to write a series set in Sunset Bay.

He wondered if he would be able to write at all.

Sitting there, everything from his past that told him he was no good, that no one would ever want him flooded over him. His parents' words forever burned into his soul, how many times had his mother told him, before she abandoned him all together, that by being born he'd ruined her life…and more sordid memories, just as hurtful that he'd kept tightly caged in the darkest corners of his soul started seeping out into his consciousness. He watched Erin, so happy and with such a perfect family and he knew he wasn't good enough for her.

He knew he could not marry her.

Slipping from the chair he walked across the sand, past the area set up for the reception and on to his car. It was time to leave.

Erin's heart was so full of happiness as she watched Brad kiss his bride. Lulu looked so happy and her joy was contagious. Everyone swamped them as soon as the kiss, the very long kiss, was done and the preacher introduced them as Mr. and Mrs. Brad Sinclair. So many friends and family gathered round and then there were wedding party photos that took a long time since she had a bunch of clowns for brothers. And cousins too. All of her girl cousins from Windswept Bay were staying with her and most of her male cousins and their wives had stayed with her brothers. While her aunt and uncle had stayed with her parents. Lulu's parents had also stayed with her parents and they'd had a great time over the weekend. Rosie told her that Marietta had told them she was expecting grandchildren very soon.

Rosie added, "I'm trying to give her what she wants but so far there is no sign of a baby Sinclair in mine and Adam's future."

"It will be when it is supposed to be," Erin told Rosie.

"And when you are supposed to have a husband who loves you it will also happen," Rosie said, hugging her. "Where is that hunky author of yours?"

"I'm not sure. I think I'll try and locate him."

"Have fun," Rosie winked as Erin smiled and went in search of Nash.

They'd finally made it to the reception and though she'd looked for him while they'd been posing for wedding pictures she hadn't found him in the crowd.

Now, she searched harder and the alarm that had been building slowly in the back of her mind began to surface. She mingled and searched for an hour before she admitted that he'd left. She told herself that it didn't mean anything as she joined in helping with the reception.

By the time she and her cousins made it home it was late.

"Where is that handsome writer guest of yours," Shar asked, pausing in the foyer, with her arm around Gage. He smiled at Erin, and she wished with all her heart that Nash would be here and she could have her arm around him and things would be as perfect and easy between them as it was between Shar and Gage.

Cali and Grant stopped halfway up the stairs. The gorgeous couple were holding hands and she loved the way the famous artist looked at her cousin. He adored her and you could tell it by the way he looked at her, the way he treated her and spoke to her. He was an amazing man who had a busy life that he juggled between being famous and living a quiet life on the shores of Windswept Bay with Cali. Erin was jealous and wished somehow Nash could come to realize that they could have what Cali and Grant had.

All of her cousins had married fantastic men. Jillian's husband, Ryan, was a police deputy and a great father to their child. And Olivia and her husband, B.J., were so cute together.

They'd all stopped at Shar's question and probably had no idea what this was doing to her. "I'm not sure. I think he left early. He might be in his room working. He often does that when he gets something on his mind." She smiled thinking about him abruptly racing up the stairs to dive into his novel. She hoped that was what he was doing right now. "You'll probably see him in the morning. But I can't promise anything. Sometimes he stays holed up for days."

Jillian smiled at her. "I think he's wonderful and you two look great together. Hopefully, we will hear some news about you two soon."

"Oh, no. Don't start thinking that."

"Of course we will." Shar laughed. "It's a perfect situation. You could advertise that you have a crazy gorgeous, famous author who inhabits your honeymoon suite. Might draw business for the other rooms."

Everyone chuckled. "Good night, cousin. See y'all in the morning. It's been so nice having you here for the weekend."

Everyone said goodnight and went to their rooms. Her heart was pounding as she looked up the flight of stairs to the third floor. Something didn't feel right.

She went back to her room and out into her garden so she could look up at the balcony and the darkness behind the glass doors. Moving back into her room she went into the kitchen and then she spotted the envelope leaning against the coffee maker. Everything in her went into slow motion. Her limbs felt heavy and her throat went dry. She stood there staring at the envelope with her name scrawled in his bold handwriting across the front.

Her fingers trembled as she reached for it. She carried it to her room and closed the door. She walked through her room and out onto her patio, surrounded by her flowers and secluded from everyone and wishing she could hear the tap of his fingers on the keyboard above her as she opened the envelope.

Erin,

Thank you for everything. I needed to leave sooner than expected. I will always remember my time in Sunset Bay.

Nash

She stared at the words. So, blunt. She blinked back tears of sorrow and anger. He would always remember his time in Sunset Bay. No, *I will remember you*. Or *our time together*. Nothing.

She loved him. *Loved* him and he hadn't even said goodbye.

Nash drove to Tampa where Natalie had chartered him a plane to New York. He was numb when he boarded the private jet and sank into the cushioned seat. He told himself he would get over this. But he felt like he'd felt after learning Gerald had died. And all during the funeral and the months afterward.

He closed his eyes as the jet sped across the

runway and lifted off and sailed into the night skies, destination New York City. He'd stay a couple of weeks maybe a month at the suite Natalie had arranged for him and he'd polish the manuscript and make everyone happy. And if he was lucky the pain in his heart and the numbness surrounding him would ease.

He hadn't told her goodbye. He knew in his heart of hearts that he had done it because he didn't want to say goodbye. But the reality was he couldn't bring himself to write the words.

Writing the words made them final and he hadn't had it in him to do it even though he knew it would have been best for Erin.

Despite it being midnight when his jet touched down, Natalie was waiting for him at the airport. Dressed in dark slacks and burgundy blazer and with her coal black hair pulled back in a clasp she looked every bit the successful literary agent that she was. At forty-five she was smart, gorgeous and one of the toughest agents in the country. And she hadn't gotten to that position because she didn't speak her mind. No, she said what she thought and pushed back when pushed.

"You look like crud," she said the moment he walked from the plane to where she waited by the SUV.

"Thanks, and it's good to see you too." He kissed her cheek, she patted him on the back as he tossed his suitcase into the open back hatch then pressed the button for it to close. He slid into the backseat and she did too.

"Hey, Harvey," he said to Natalie's longtime driver.

"Hi, Mr. Bond. And she's right, you look terrible. Are you not sleeping?"

"You two are a barrel of laughs. I've had a long night, and no, I didn't sleep on the plane."

"I don't sleep on them either. I'll have you at your hotel soon." Harvey then slid the window between the front seat and the rear seats closed giving him and Natalie privacy.

"Why did you leave early?"

"It was time to leave."

Natalie studied him. "You seemed to do really well there. Looking at you now, I'm a little shocked. You look haggard. I thought you'd look rested and excited like you used to when you finished a book. Before…your dad died."

He stared out the window at the lights of the city. "I thought so too. I'll start on the polish of the manuscript after I get some rest."

"Great. We have a new contract offer. They're wanting the next three installments of the series. Your fans love this Clayburn character and I think—"

"There won't be any more of them. This was the last. I told you before, Nat. I'm moving on."

"I understand you're getting bored with the character but the advance is—"

"I don't care what the advance is. Nat, I almost didn't get this book written. I thought it was because of my grief over losing my dad. And it was partly, but it was also I realized when I was in Sunset Bay that something inside of me changed and I want to explore a new idea." His thoughts were all back in Sunset Bay with the new characters he'd been tossing around in his head and the real people who inspired them. And especially with Erin…who—he closed his eyes…she didn't inspire his work, she inspired him.

He closed his eyes and saw her face. He could only imagine what she felt when she read his note. His cowardly, stupid note. His heart ached as if it had been kicked. *I'm not good enough for her*. He heard the words, but maybe it was because he was so tired, or missing her so much, wanting her so badly that they didn't ring true. Why was he letting the people who had hurt him the most in life have the most power over him?

He loved Erin and he knew in his heart that he would never do anything to hurt her. *But you have already hurt her.*

"What's up, Nash? You're my client but also my friend. I've been worried about you. But you seemed better in Sunset Bay. Nash, talk to me."

He took her hand and gave it a gentle squeeze. "I

don't think I've ever told you how grateful I am for your friendship. I am. And I think I've made a mistake. Now, let's turn this SUV around and get me back on a flight to Sunset Bay." He tapped on the window and Harvey pushed a button to open the window.

"Sir?"

"Turn around please. I need back on that plane."

CHAPTER SIXTEEN

By noon her cousins had headed back home and she was supposed to have lunch at her parent's home with Lulu and Brad and all of her family before they left for their honeymoon in Kauai. She walked the distance, surprised by how calm she was. Nash had been invited to the honeymoon send-off too and now she would have a lot of questions to answer.

She'd known this was coming but the anger she felt at how he'd ended it was like a fist knotted around her windpipe. He hadn't even said goodbye.

Her family was all here, the driveway was full of

cars. Brad's Jeep was on the street ready to take them to the airport. She had to be pleasant and not let the hurt and anger show. She would not let the hurt tear her apart and the anger helped her succeed at that.

"You're here," Cassie called, waving her over to the kitchen counter. "Can you help finish up this tray of veggies."

"Good morning, dear," her mother came and gave her a hug. "The wedding was so beautiful last night. Did you ever find Nash?" She looked behind Erin then back at her. "Is he with you?"

"Hey, sis," Jonah said, coming in and swiping a carrot stick from the veggie tray. "You look terrible. Did you stay up all night? You and Nash go dancing or something?" He smiled and took a bite of the carrot.

"No, he left. Had to go back to New York early."

"Oh," Cassie said, caution in her words.

"Is he coming back?" Jonah asked. "He said he wanted to take the boat out again this week."

"No, I don't think he's coming back."

"Oh, honey. I'm so sorry." Marietta slipped her arms around Erin and hugged her. Erin fought the tears that this caused. Her mother had suspected or hoped that something was going on between them.

Stepping back Erin sniffed and wiped her tears, and caught Jonah's stormy expression.

"Did he hurt you?"

"Depends on what you mean. He didn't mean to hurt me. I'm fine."

More people gathered in the kitchen. So much of their lives had taken place in this kitchen. Family events, talks, tears. Comfort and hugs. Good food, laughter and joy.

"I heard," Lulu said, coming to hug her. "I'm so sorry," she whispered in her ear. "If you need to talk I'm here for another few days before the honeymoon."

"No way," Erin whispered back. "You are not to worry about my love life right now."

"Then I will, you come talk to me if you need to." Rosie said hugging her.

These two knew exactly what she was feeling, and how deep the hurt went. She blinked, and forced her tears away. "I'm fine. I knew this was coming."

Her family filtered into the large space, each

hearing the news that Nash had left and taken Erin's heart with him.

"He was a good guy," Jonah said.

Tate's expression was hard. "Yeah, but I'm not liking that he left the way he did. Erin deserved an explanation."

"He didn't strike me as a coward," Brad said, placing an arm across Lulu's shoulders. "Something about this doesn't ring right."

"I didn't suspect it either," her dad said. He looked like he would join Tate and Brad in finding Nash. The fact that her family had her back was touching and reassuring.

Adam crossed his arms and looked like he was thinking hard about something. "Did he have to go back? There are a lot of reasons he may have left early. I'm not ready to jump to conclusions. He just seemed like a great fella and you two seemed to hit it off. Maybe he's going to surprise you and come back."

She didn't want to ruin Adam's hopeful conviction that Nash hadn't left her for good so she just smiled. Feeling completely distracted.

By the time she made it back home she had put on a good show, but inside she felt numb and grief for what she had hoped for and lost was setting in. She wanted to hole up in her room alone and just not move for a few days.

She had lost him.

When she opened the door to the house she halted, the scent of something delicious wafted in from the kitchen and there was soft music playing. Her heart started beating rapidly and she walked slowly toward the kitchen. The only thought she had was that Nash had come back. But why would he be cooking?

She walked into the kitchen and her breath caught. The kitchen table had been covered with a white tablecloth, there were candles flickering from candlesticks, and flowers, a beautiful array of red roses in the center of the table. And Nash stood beside the table looking tired, but wonderful in dress slacks and shirt.

"I thought I'd try my hand at setting a romantic table for you. What do you think?"

She walked closer. "It's beautiful and so very

romantic," her voice came out barely above a whisper. "But, why did you come back?"

He took her hands in his and her pulse went wild. "Because I couldn't leave. You see, I've always been missing something in my life, something that even after my dad rescued me and loved me there was something missing that not even he could fill with all the love he gave me. After he died I was like a boat adrift at sea, I lost the only person who ever loved me, cared for me and I struggled to even find words, much less my way. But the moment I entered the doors of this house, I found my words again, but more important, when I came here I found my heart also. And now that I've found you I can't function without you nor do I want to. You are my heart, Erin Sinclair. The part of me that's always been missing."

She trembled at his words, her knees melting as he knelt before her, looking up at her with his dear, gorgeous face and earnest eyes so full of love for her. Tears seeped from her eyes. "Nash?" she whispered through the tears.

"Erin, sweetheart, you know how I told you I was

getting parts of the new story idea after we talked that night about the table setting? I realized last night after I landed in New York that the new story idea set here in Sunset Bay, the one that was building in my mind and taking over my thoughts…was my love story. Our love story. It wasn't a fictional book idea but the story of my future here in this town, with me putting down roots with you. I've come back to ask you to marry me. Will you marry me, Erin?"

Her heart was so full it was probably going to explode.

How had this happened?

He'd come back for her. He loved her. Her heart ached with love and longing for him.

She sank to sit on his knee because her own wouldn't hold her up any longer and she cupped his jaw with her hand. "I love you too, Nash. Yes, I'll marry you. Yes, and we'll live this love story together." And she met his lips with hers as his arms went around her and he lifted her in his arms, holding her close as they kissed.

After a moment he pulled back, his heart

thundering against hers and his hands tightening, holding her as close as he could get her. "I'm not easy to live with, but I'll work on that and love you forever."

She smiled, loving him so much. "You are a quick learner, just look at this table. It is amazing and romantic and I have no doubt that we're going to manage together just fine."

He laughed. "I'm counting on it," he said, his voice gruff, tenderness filled his eyes. "I love you, Erin, heart of mine. I've been longing for your love all my life and now that I have you, I'll treasure you for the rest of my life."

And then he kissed her again and she knew in his arms was where she'd always longed to be.

EPILOGUE

Jonah knocked on Erin's door and waited for his sister to answer. He was worried about her. She'd been quiet at his parent's house and he knew more than any of his family that she'd fallen for Nash. He'd seen them almost kissing on the pier that day and he'd rented the boat to them that evening. He'd seen the way they looked at each other and he truly thought Nash cared for her. So he was as baffled as she was about why he'd left. He had come to ask questions away from the family. He needed to know if he needed to make a trip to New York and confront the man. Not that Jonah was a violent man, despite his size he'd never been a fighter but if this guy had come to their small town and messed with his sister's heart and then walked away with no remorse…Jonah was going to go have a talk with Nash Bond.

The door opened and Erin stood there smiling. She was flushed and completely not the same person he'd seen an hour ago at his parent's house.

"Jonah. Hi."

"Hey, I stopped by to see if you were okay. I was worried about you. But you…you don't look upset any more. Is everything okay?"

She smiled and then he heard footsteps behind her and the door opened wider and there stood Nash.

"Hey, Jonah, I'm glad you came by to check on Erin."

"What's going on?" he asked, looking from his sister's smiling face to Nash's serious face. "You left. And Erin was pretty shook up."

Nash pulled Erin into his arms and looked into her eyes, that look of love on his expression that Jonah had been pretty certain he'd seen before. Maybe even before they'd realized it.

"I'm so sorry you were so shook up that your family was upset for you."

She kissed him gently and then smiled at Jonah. "Nash was here waiting for me. He asked me to marry him and I said yes. You are officially the first to know."

Relief washed over him. For his sister and for the fact that he'd really liked Nash and hadn't wanted to think badly of him. He'd come through after all and that made Jonah extremely happy. "Congratulations. I thought you two were in love. I was planning on coming to see you in New York." He grinned when Nash hefted a thick brow. "Yeah, to find out why you came and broke my sister's heart."

"Good for you. I like that you were looking out for her. But don't worry, because I'm crazy about your sister and plan on proving it to her for the rest of my life." Nash held his hand out to shake Jonah's.

Jonah shook and then when Nash kissed Erin again, he said, "Well, I see my work here is done. I'll let you two have some time alone. Congratulations again. Mom will be over the moon happy."

They broke the kiss and Erin chuckled. "Yes, she will be. One by one we are making her day. How much longer are you going to hold out?"

He gave a small smile. "Like I'm always saying, I'm in no rush. When the right one comes along I'll be ready."

He was smiling when he left the lovebirds, happy for them. He walked down the street and toward the pier. This called for an ice cream cone. He loved ice cream and used anything and everything as an excuse to grab a cone. Besides that, he enjoyed people watching at the pier.

A few minutes later he had his cone, and was busy enjoying it watching all the people and trying not to think about how the right woman didn't seem to be in his future. He'd grown weary of looking for her. Endless dates that ended with him feeling down, and constantly having to push himself to go on another date only to realize pretty quickly that this one wasn't her either.

Lately, it had become harder and harder for him to

make himself ask anyone out. He leaned against the railing not too far from the ice cream truck and licked his cone watching the people enjoying their afternoon. Today there seemed to be couples everywhere reminding him that he was here alone and feeling slightly dissatisfied. He had a good life. A great business and most of the time a positive attitude. But more and more he was feeling lonely…so what was he going to do about that?

Was he ready to jump back into the dating pool?

More Books by Debra Clopton

Turner Creek Ranch Series
Treasure Me, Cowboy (Book 1)
Rescue Me, Cowboy (Book 2)
Complete Me, Cowboy (Book 3)
Sweet Talk Me, Cowboy (Book 4)

Texas Matchmaker Series
Dream With Me, Cowboy (Book 1)
Be My Love, Cowboy (Book 2)
This Heart's Yours, Cowboy (Book 3)
Hold Me, Cowboy (Book 4)
Be Mine, Cowboy (Book 5)
Marry Me, Cowboy (Book 6)
Cherish Me, Cowboy (Book 7)
Surprise Me, Cowboy (Book 8)
Serenade Me, Cowboy (Book 9)
Return To Me, Cowboy (Book 10)
Love Me, Cowboy (Book 11)
Ride With Me, Cowboy (Book 12)
Dance With Me, Cowboy (Book 13)

Windswept Bay Series
From This Moment On (Book 1)
Somewhere With You (Book 2)
With This Kiss (Book 3)
Forever and For Always (Book 4)
Holding Out For Love (Book 5)
With This Ring (Book 6)
With This Promise (Book 7)
With This Pledge (Book 8)
With This Wish (Book 9)
With This Forever (Book 10)
With This Vow (Book 11)

About the Author

Bestselling author Debra Clopton has sold over 2.5 million books. Her book OPERATION: MARRIED BY CHRISTMAS has been optioned for an ABC Family Movie. Debra is known for her contemporary, western romances, Texas cowboys and feisty heroines. Sweet romance and humor are always intertwined to make readers smile. A sixth generation Texan she lives with her husband on a ranch deep in the heart of Texas. She loves being contacted by readers.

Visit Debra's website at www.debraclopton.com

Sign up for Debra's newsletter at www.debraclopton.com/contest/

Check out her Facebook at www.facebook.com/debra.clopton.5

Follow her on Twitter at @debraclopton

Contact her at debraclopton@ymail.com

If you enjoyed reading *Longing for Love* I would appreciate it if you would help others enjoy this book, too.

Recommend it. Please help other readers find this book by recommending it to friends, reader's groups and discussion boards.

Review it. Please tell other readers why you liked this book by reviewing it on the retail site you purchased it from or Goodreads. If you do write a review, please send an email to debraclopton@ymail.com so I can thank you with a personal email. Or visit me at: www.debraclopton.com.